'The strength here is truly in the minimalist prose — razor-sharp sentences that often slot together perfectly in a seemingly nonchalant way. The result is a powerful story about death, life, and survival.'

Nederlands Dagblad

'It is impossible to name everything that is beautiful about this novel. Posthuma needs few words to evoke a feeling or an atmosphere. She writes striking sentences that conjure up poignant images ... this book deserves a large readership.'

Literary Netherlands

'What makes *What I'd Rather Not Think About* rise above the average mourning novel is its utter authenticity. Posthuma associates, philosophises, links memories to everyday actions, draws on films and television series, and tries to interpret in a laconic, light-footed, and pointed way. "Less is more" with Jente Posthuma. And again, she seems to be saying: nothing is "whole" here, in the subhuman. Everything rumbles, frays, and creaks.'

The Telegraph

'From the opening pages of this novel I had no idea where it was going, but I trusted Posthuma completely. Tender, offbeat, and deftly drawn — I loved it.'

Allee Richards, author of *The Small Joys of Real Life*

'A unique story of a twin brother and sister, wryly funny and heartbreakingly sad. Her characters desperately try to make sense of our ever more complex world. This is a rare book. And Jente Posthuma is a treasure and a hell of a writer.'

Herman Koch, international bestselling author of *The Dinner*

what I'd rather not think about

what I'd rather not think about

Jente Posthuma

Translated by Sarah Timmer Harvey

SCRIBE

Melbourne | London | Minneapolis

Scribe Publications
18–20 Edward St, Brunswick, Victoria 3056, Australia
2 John St, Clerkenwell, London, WC1N 2ES, United Kingdom
3754 Pleasant Ave, Suite 100, Minneapolis, Minnesota 55409, USA

First published in Dutch as *Waar ik liever niet aan denk* by Pluim in 2020
Published by Scribe 2023
Reprinted 2024

Typeset in Adobe Garamond by the publishers.

Printed and bound in the UK by CPI Group (UK) Ltd,
Croydon CR0 4YY

Scribe is committed to the sustainable use of natural resources and the use of paper products made responsibly from those resources.

978 1 922585 80 6 (Australian edition)
978 1 914484 71 1 (UK edition)
978 1 957363 35 6 (US edition)
978 1 761385 13 1 (ebook)

Catalogue records for this book are available from the National Library of Australia and the British Library.

This project has been assisted by the Australian Government through the Australia Council, its arts funding and advisory body.

scribepublications.com.au
scribepublications.co.uk
scribepublications.com

For Jampiejoris

and he knew then that Roy had loved him and that that should have been enough. He just hadn't understood anything in time.

David Vann, *Legend of a Suicide*, 2008

Waterboarding, I told my mother. It's when someone places a cloth over your face, then continuously pours water over it. It feels like drowning. It *is* drowning.

And you're going to do it, she said.

Yes.

My mother sighed. This has to be one of your brother's ideas.

We'd just seen a film about Guantanamo Bay, I said. Afterwards, he asked if I could waterboard him, he wants to know how it feels, and I said I'd only do it if he did it to me too. So, that's how it came about.

And how was it? My mother asked.

We haven't done it yet!

As my mother grew older, her listening skills had become even worse.

Oh yes, she said. I was watching a show on television yesterday, and one of my favourite characters was blown up, which is why I slept so poorly.

We felt we should be able to lie in a reasonably comfortable position, so we decided to do it on my couch. My brother went first. He lay on his back with a red checked dishcloth draped over his face. I stood next to him with a jug of water.

Here we go, I said, pouring water over the cloth. After a few seconds, my brother pulled the cloth off his face and sat up.

Maybe we should tie you up, I said.

I tied his wrists together with one of my stockings and started again. We agreed that I would remove the cloth after thirty seconds and set a timer on my phone. My brother gasped and tried to move his arms. He's drowning, I thought. It took a long time for thirty seconds to pass and once I'd lifted the cloth away from his face and he'd finished coughing, he said: That's enough.

I didn't want my wrists bound, I wanted to be able to pull the cloth off my face whenever it suited me.

That's not how this works, my brother said. He tied the stocking around my wrists and put the cloth over my face. The water ran into my nose, and I couldn't breathe. I tried to get up and knocked something over with my leg. Once I was finally upright, I shook the wet cloth off my face and wrenched my hands free.

My brother handed me a tissue to wipe my face but I shook my head, breathing in and out, over and over again. Church bells rang, the alarm on my phone went off.

Why didn't you help me?

Sorry, he said.

I felt like I was going to throw up. I hung my head over the toilet and waited for something to come out but nothing did and

I thought about the time I'd taken a guy home and the way he'd pushed my head down. His hands had covered my ears and he kept pushing my head lower, and maybe he thought it was turning me on because when I pressed against his knees and tried to break free, he gripped me even tighter, and all I could hear was my thumping heart. And then I thought about the first time I'd heard someone say their heart was in their throat. My mother had been the one to say it. She told someone that her heart was in her throat whenever she thought about what the future held for her daughter because I was no great beauty. She didn't worry about my brother and how he was always plucking his hair, or about the bald patch his plucking caused. I can't remember when he stopped plucking but he was done with it after a while, and his hair grew back.

My son is good at everything, my mother often said. One day, he's going to do something extraordinary.

After my brother was born again during a workshop, he said: Life isn't a straight line. It's a circle. You can die and start over again.

The workshop was organised by Osho's followers, who, twenty years after his death, still viewed him as a spiritual master, which was also the meaning of his name.

Osho, said my brother. You know who that is, right? The man who used to call himself Bhagwan, which means God.

Of course I knew exactly who he meant. He was talking about the man who was born Chandra Mohan, a common name in India but when he was a child, his grandparents had called him Rajneesh, which means King of the Night. Rajneesh would often go to the river close to his hometown, push the other children underwater until they were on the verge of drowning and then ask them how it felt. As the Bhagwan, he'd said: *Hope is a drug. Only those who are prepared to die will know a life full of love. Those who are afraid of death will never penetrate the mystery of love.* He told the people who came to his Ashram in Poona that they needed to surrender themselves. *If you walk away now*, he said, *you might as well end your life.* According to him, the urge to kill yourself was a sign of true intelligence and sensitivity, a desire to escape the suffocation of the ego. For those who recognised the pointlessness of everything, suicide — or total surrender — was the only alternative. This is more or less what was posted on one of my brother's favourite websites, in short, oddly fragmented sentences, all lined up like a bad poem.

The cause of Osho's death in 1990 is unclear, as he was cremated a few hours after he died. Just before he died, Osho claimed to have been poisoned while serving time in an American prison in 1985. There are those who believe he'd simply grown tired of living and had asked his personal physician to administer a lethal injection.

Later, my brother stopped believing life was circular. We're at the beginning of an extreme weather episode, he said. From here on out, it will only get worse.

In a national study on happiness, our hometown scored just above average. Or just below average, I don't quite remember anymore. In any case, I have fond memories of our town but my brother did not. Right until the very end, he'd get annoyed if I mentioned the fountain in the town square and the children who played there, the smaller ones naked and the older ones in bathing suits, or if I brought up the pink glitter bikini that my aunt had brought me back from New York.

In 1990, the year my brother and I turned ten, and the year of my glitter bikini, there were 2,245 murders in New York. And 596 suicides. It was also the year that a couple of the boys at the fountain made a habit of pulling off my brother's swimming trunks, so he'd be forced to walk home naked.

New York does have suicide-free days. These aren't holidays, it isn't as if they're announced in advance. July 12, 1993, was a suicide-free day in New York. My brother and I read about it the following afternoon on the teletext news. We'd just returned from the parking lot behind the supermarket, where there was an enormous crane. It's probably fifty metres high, said my brother. What would it be like to climb all the way to the top, I said. How far would you be able to see. A motorbike revved noisily behind me, and I turned to see one of the employees from the meat section tearing out of the lot. All the noise that motorbikes make, my brother used to say, is entirely unnecessary, it's all for show. When I turned back, my brother was already halfway up the crane. I quickly looked at the ground, staring at the clumps of grass beside my feet until my neck began to hurt and my brother finally jumped off the crane and landed back beside me with a thud. You can see the city, he said, and all the bends the river makes on its way there.

Was it beautiful?

It was mainly just far, he said.

And right before we fell asleep that night, he said: Today was another suicide-free day.

Between 2000 and 2015, the number of murders in New York decreased significantly but the number of suicides rose. The most popular ways of committing suicide in New York are hanging, asphyxiation or jumping from a great height. While the number of jumpers is declining, New York still has more jumpers than the rest of the United States. Eight times more, to be exact.

Perhaps New York owes its high number of jumpers to Wall Street, where every now and then, in times of recession, a hedge fund manager will jump out a window. According to the Centers for Disease Control and Prevention, people who work on Wall Street are forty per cent more likely to take their own life than the average person. Wall Street professionals are by nature competitive perfectionists — their work is their identity, and they constantly compare themselves to their colleagues.

My brother called himself One and me Two because he had been born forty-five minutes earlier than I was on a sweltering day in August. He treated me like his little sister, was longer and heavier than me at birth, and had taken up almost all the space in my mother's belly. I'd been stuck behind him with my left leg thrown over my shoulder, or so the story goes. This was why it took a little extra time for me to emerge. Our actual due date had been a month later but my brother had gone ahead, and I wasn't about to be left behind.

The fact that we weren't identical was something I'd long considered a handicap, a consequence of our premature birth, even once I understood the difference between identical and fraternal twins. We could have grown even closer in that ninth month.

My brother was more active, talked louder and threw bigger tantrums than I did. He hurled things, slammed doors and kicked holes in them. After these fits, he would lock himself in his room and when he eventually came back downstairs, he'd act as if nothing had happened. All my parents needed to do was watch him and occasionally repair something. They were forced to give me their attention. I insisted they comfort me whenever I was upset and refused to let their gaze wander to the newspaper or television. This was back when I still wore my feelings on the outside, like a coat, and didn't understand that this wasn't something you were supposed to do.

Demanding was the word they used to describe me. They called my brother headstrong. He always knew everything better than I did. I don't think I ever heard him respond with *Oh, yeah?*

9

or *Wow, I didn't know that*, when I told him something. He usually said, *I know*, and if there was something he didn't know, then he would say nothing.

The North Tower was called 1 WTC, so the South Tower was called 2 WTC. 1 WTC was 417 metres high, and 2 WTC was two metres shorter. 1 WTC had an antenna on the roof and was completed in 1972, a year earlier than 2 WTC, which did not have an antenna. For a short while, 1 WTC was the tallest building in the world, until Chicago's 442-metre-high Sears Tower surpassed it in 1973. This was a bitter pill for 1 WTC to swallow but what is worse? To have briefly been the tallest building in the world or never to have been the tallest because the building next to you was always slightly taller.

I used to sleep with a Continental Airlines poster above my bed. It was an image of the Twin Towers set against the pink evening light. Compared to the towers, the Statue of Liberty appeared minuscule in the foreground. Liberty looked like she was trying to set the towers on fire with her torch. I bought the poster at the flea market I went to every Saturday with my father. When I came home with it, my brother said, That photo is inaccurate. In reality, the towers aren't the same height.

I dreamed of seeing the towers up close. I didn't need to go inside them and certainly didn't want to go to the top, though standing underneath the towers could also be risky. Ever since a famous pop star had jumped out of a hotel window in the city closest to our town, and we learned from our mother that the self-inflicted death of a celebrity was usually followed by a wave of copycat suicides, we would look up at the top of every tall building we passed to see if there were any jumpers.

Our parents were geologists, so they looked at the ground a lot. They both worked at the Geological Institute in the city. My mother was an expert in landslides, and my father did microscopic soil research. Whenever there was any dirt that needed excavating, my brother and I had to list the various layers of soil we observed. During our vacations in Sweden, we were constantly hacking away at the ground, searching for fossils that were at least 350 million years old. My parents didn't think anything younger than that was worth the trouble. I collected minerals and fossils, not because I thought they were beautiful but because my mother also collected them. She displayed the most interesting specimens in every available corner of the house. The rest were stored in boxes underneath her bed, where my collection also ended up once I grew tired of it.

My brother collected comic books, and my father collected old biscuit tins. One of the walls in the shed was covered entirely with tins that held all my father's screws and nails. He didn't organise the tins by their contents but by colour, just like the layers of soil on the geological chart on the opposite wall: every layer was a different earth tone. I enjoyed being in the shed, looking at the colours and my father's back as he opened tin after tin, searching for the right nail. My father also liked hanging out in the shed — presumably for the colours, because he wasn't much of a handyman. Though he acted like he was, in the same way he pretended to be a fun dad.

We discovered that we were attracted to boys when we were eight and both fell in love with Hans. He had dark-blond highlighted hair and a perfect face. I was primarily attracted to the way his hair fell over his green eyes, and his warm voice. My brother loved his eyes and white teeth. Hans was a presenter, he hosted television programmes. We were allowed to watch him on television every evening after dinner. When I looked at Hans and he looked at me, I no longer felt like a girl. I felt like a woman.

Hans isn't into women, said my brother one day. We were lying on our stomachs on the carpet, watching him. Hans is gay, he said, just a little too loudly. Our mother had told him so. I called out to her but she didn't come. I went into the kitchen, where she was doing the dishes, and asked her about Hans.

Gay, she said. He has a boyfriend.

I ran back to the living room.

He's seeing someone, I told my brother, casually as I could.

It took another eight years for my brother to tell our mother that he was into boys, a fact so obvious to me that his solemn tone seemed absurd. My brother was the norm, and I was the anomaly, which is why I didn't understand my mother's odd reaction. She acted like it was something she needed to absolve. It's not a big deal was all she said. Just like the time he'd accidentally broken a fossilised turd from her collection, and she'd spent the entire weekend bent over her desk in the study, sticking the pieces back together with special glue.

Maybe it was because he'd been a relentless know-it-all or perhaps it was due to his disinterest in the only girl in our class who had breasts but in the fifth grade, just after the Christmas holidays, all my brother's friends turned against him. They called him names and got frozen dog shit from the bushes outside to put on his chair at school. They would kick him and try to trip him while we were walking home. Why don't you hit back? I often asked him, and in response he'd just shrug.

Almost a year later, in December, the bullying suddenly stopped. We don't know why it stopped, even my brother had no idea. My mother said we should see it as a natural phenomenon, like a storm that surges, then dies down again. This would make it easier for us to accept it, along with the devastation left in its wake.

The day the Twin Towers fell, I was watching a rerun of a talk show when the programme was interrupted by a news bulletin. A plane had ploughed into one of the towers and I immediately thought of my brother because I always think of my brother when something important happens.

When we turned eighteen, we moved to Amsterdam together. Both of us rented apartments on the park, him on the east side and me on the west, 300 metres away, close to the main entrance. According to my brother, all the park entrances were equally important.

It was the first time either of us had lived alone. Although, I did eat dinner at my brother's place five times a week because I wasn't fond of cooking. In return, he could always count on me to do his laundry. I studied English and had a part-time job in a vintage clothing shop. My brother also studied English and worked at a gay bar. He liked it so much that after a couple of months, he quit his studies and went to work at the bar full-time.

By the time I called him, he'd already heard the news.

The tower, I said. Have you seen it?

While we were talking, a plane flew into the second tower. We watched TV with our phones glued to our ears for the rest of the day, surfing from channel to channel.

This is bad, my brother kept saying. People are jumping out of windows. They're jumping.

He was crying, and the shock of this silenced me, because my brother never cried.

The first sweater I bought with my own money was nice and warm and made of Icelandic wool. It wasn't as soft as some of the sweaters I'd buy once I started working at the vintage shop, when one of my bedroom walls would gradually disappear behind a mountain of wool. I hung shelves from the floor to the ceiling and filled them with piles of sweaters, which, just like my father's biscuit tins, were sorted according to colour. By my twenty-seventh birthday, I owned 142 sweaters, and it was high time I saw a therapist. *What will you do with them all,* my friends would say. *It's a collection,* I'd tell them. I didn't have any pets, so I stroked my sweaters whenever I had nothing else to do.

I also sourced almost all of my brother's clothes at the shop. Underpants, socks and tank tops were the only things he bought himself. We were like French film stars, walking down the street in our sweaters. People turned to look at us. This was before he developed a paunch and dark circles under his eyes.

After a few months of therapy, the Christmas holidays were upon us and I wondered if I should give Elza, my therapist, an end-of-year gift. Technically, she did work for me but I wasn't her boss. I decided to bring her two identical Christmas sweaters for her granddaughters, twins with large, earnest eyes, whom I occasionally met in the hallway.

Elza was sixty-two and had recently retired when I started seeing her but she still saw some clients at her home. My work is never done, she said. After our intake session, she told me, I can help you develop a more positive self-image but you have a long road ahead. (I'm now one of her three remaining clients. I've never run into the other two and don't know if my road is longer than theirs.)

When I gave her the sweaters, we were sitting upstairs in her office while the twins played downstairs under the watchful eyes of their other grandmother. Elza and her wife were looking after the kids during the day until they were old enough to attend school.

How lovely, Elza said.

For the girls, I said.

She put the sweaters on her lap and stroked the wool. Both her hand and the sweaters remained in her lap for the rest of our session.

At thirteen, I was already over six feet tall and, on the advice of my mother and the internist, taking hormones to stunt my growth. My brother didn't need to take them. He was taller than me but people never said to him, *You're so tall*, or, *Can we guess your height? We've taken bets on it*. I did my best to shrink myself in every possible way. I was athletic and a good student but careful not to excel at anything, because that way I would have more friends. Whenever I was in a good mood and happened to be the centre of attention, I'd feel ashamed afterwards. Yet my brother was always praised for putting himself out there, especially during PE, so he'd get up an hour earlier than me to do sit-ups and lift weights. While I was doing my best to shrink, he kept getting bigger. During our final year of school, he bulked up so much that our class teacher saw him as a leader and asked if he would manage the finances for the graduation party. My brother bought an enormous disco ball with the money he collected from the class, after that there was only enough left over for ten jumbo-sized packets of value-brand chips, and everyone had to bring their own drinks. Our teacher kept an eye on all the drinks, immediately confiscating any alcohol we tried to smuggle into the party. I'd hidden a bottle in a secret pocket in my bag and was able to sneak covert sips from it. My brother got caught with his bottle early on and spent the rest of the evening dancing angrily under the disco ball, while I drank the rest of my vodka behind the thick curtains in the auditorium and let myself get fingered by a boy who also happened to be standing there.

$\mathbb{S}$ ylvia Plath prepared bread and milk for her children and then stuck her head in the oven. Her daughter, Frieda, was almost three, and her son, Nicholas, had just turned one.

I read *The Bell Jar* for my Modern English Literature class and it had impressed me. After everything I'd heard, I was expecting a dense, sappy story but was surprised by the novel's light tone. My brother read it too — purely out of interest because he'd quit his studies six months earlier — and had been similarly impressed but was also a little critical.

He said it was brave of her to take her mother's pills and hide in the crawl space at her parents' house but it hadn't been particularly smart.

I said that he shouldn't conflate the protagonist with the author. He said I was naïve and that he'd never, ever use painkillers to end his life. The risk of failure was too great.

I told him about Sylvia's friend, the poet Anne Sexton, who had put on her mother's fur coat, poured herself a glass of vodka, and gone to the garage, where she'd started the car and died of carbon monoxide poisoning. Her daughters were twenty-one and nineteen. And another poet, Ingrid Jonker, who'd walked into the sea in Cape Town. Her daughter, Simone, had been eleven. My brother said he would never have kids and then kick the bucket. Isn't that what happens to every parent eventually, I said. He didn't think that was funny. It's a crime, he said, to have a child only to leave it. Of course, we both knew he was talking about our father, a man who'd left us shortly after our eleventh birthday because he no longer loved our mother and wanted to study mud in the Amazon region. He died suddenly from a brain aneurysm during one of his expeditions through the rainforest.

Sylvia Plath's son, Nicholas Hughes, also killed himself, I said. He hung himself.

Did he have any children?

This I didn't know.

He was a marine biologist, I said. A salmon expert.

I was pleased that I had the facts for once, while my brother was the one with the questions. I could also tell him about Ted Hughes' girlfriend, Assia Wevill, who killed herself in almost the same way as his wife, Sylvia Plath. Assia had taken her four-year-old daughter's life too. My brother was getting wound up.

Virginia Woolf didn't have any children, I added quickly.

Let's watch some TV, he said. I'm in the mood for a stupid game show. He went into the living room and sat on the couch.

I also knew that Virginia Woolf had put on a fur coat, filled the pockets with stones and drowned herself in a river. Just like my brother but I didn't know this at the time.

S uicide is an aggressive act, Elza recently said. If you're capable of ending your own life, then you must at least have the capacity for violence.

Have you ever punched anyone in the face? I like to ask people this question. Most say they haven't. I've never done it either but I have had a fist hit my face. It was my brother's fist, when we were twelve. It was a reflex, he said afterwards. He was sorry. I shouldn't have touched his computer or pressed the enter key so much and so hard. You could have damaged it, he said. He also thought I should apologise but I refused.

Elza said that while she'd obviously never met my brother, based on my stories, she was able to conclude that my brother couldn't control his anger, and this was problematic.

Especially during our childhood, I said. But that was the only time he ever hit me. He could certainly curse, and he threw things, like his laptop, when he got older, even though he was crazy about computers and wouldn't let anyone touch his laptop. Totally inconsistent, I said. Elza asked if I was still angry at him, and I shook my head wildly.

The first time I heard the word Mengele, I was eight. The radio was on. My mother liked to listen to the news on Sunday afternoons. I was on the shag carpet beside the window, lying in the sun like a cat, slowly drifting away on a river of words. I could picture the grassy riverbank ahead and had just put my legs in the water when one word suddenly pulled me under. *Mengele*, said a dark voice on the radio, and it made me think of the water beneath a thick layer of ice. If you found yourself trapped under ice, I'd heard that it was best to look for light because that's where you were likely to find a gap. Or else it was the other way around, I kept forgetting, and it worried me that if it ever came to it, I wouldn't be able to choose between the darkness and the light. My father said light, my brother said dark, and my mother didn't seem to care.

It was only later that I understood Mengele was a name that belonged to someone, a person with neatly trimmed hair who had died in the warm Brazilian sea a year and a half before I was born. Staring at the photo of him in my history book, at the gap between his teeth, I kept thinking about the ice and the cold and the breathlessness and vowed never to go to Brazil, the country where Mengele had ended up after fleeing from the secret service and where my father had gone when he'd fled from us.

Did you know that Mossad tried to cosy up to Mengele's second ex-wife Martha in 1961? I asked Elza. They wanted to use her to discover his whereabouts. Unfortunately, the journalist who was supposed to initiate an affair with her had failed to consider that she was a foot taller than him, which made a romantic relationship between them impossible. At least, this is what was written in the report released by Mossad.

No, Elza said. No, I didn't know that.

Do you remember that comedian who was always on TV on Sundays? I asked. He once said during an interview that he thought being tall was trashy. But I'd rather be tall than big. Luckily, I'm not big.

What's the difference? Elza asked.

Big means large, substantial.

What's wrong with being large and substantial?

Elza was small and lean, like my mother. My mother always called herself petite, never small.

That's what Leo always says, I answered. My boyfriend. He's smaller than me.

I'd only just met him. This was before we were married.

In the years after graduation, I continued working at the vintage clothing shop, much to my mother's chagrin because it dashed her dream of having one of her children pursue a career in academia. I'd just pulled a sweater onto my lap when Leo wandered into the shop. I was stroking the sweater, which he later told me he found quite calming. Trying on clothes made him nervous because he usually wore overalls to work. Leo restored and sold

old furniture. Occasionally, he was asked to design a kitchen or wooden staircase.

Wood is so welcoming, he often said. It's a fact.

I walked through the shop to get him a pair of pants and frowned when I spotted my reflection in the mirror.

Do you always look so angry when you catch sight of yourself, he asked, then smiled at me in the mirror with those eyes. I can still remember the way he looked at me. This was a man for whom I wouldn't have to shrink myself, this was someone who had enough space.

If you tell yourself, I'm going to remember this moment for the rest of my life, then you will remember it. You have to focus on your thoughts while simultaneously absorbing everything around you but if you do this, then the moment will stay with you forever, no matter how insignificant it may seem. I can still picture myself sitting on a terrace beside a canal with my mother, bags of newly bought clothes sitting between our legs. I was happy with my new white Nikes and oversized yellow sweater. My mother was drinking sherry and I had a beer. It wasn't a particularly memorable moment but I still recall exactly how the light fell and our view over the canal and the sunglasses my mother was wearing, all because I'd decided to remember that moment and probably also because it wasn't often that my mother would free up an entire Saturday afternoon to spend time with me. That morning she'd gone to her walking club but cancelled her afternoon gardening club meeting so she could visit me in the city.

Your life will slip away if you don't share it with anyone, she said. And I'd explained how you could hold onto a moment. But you can't use it to hold onto people, I said, because they can always just get up and walk out of view.

That's not so bad, my mother said. It doesn't have to be a bad thing. If you always keep this in mind, then it won't be so bad.

remember places but not the roads I've taken to get there. I don't recall driving to the village to see my brother's body but I do remember him lying underneath a sheet on a table in the morgue, and the plastic bag full of wet clothes my mother held in both hands, which had pulled her shoulders into a slight hunch. And his green striped sweater. I could still remember the birthday when I'd given it to him. We were sitting on a terrace at the botanical gardens when he asked if it was a sweater for posh people. He seemed to like this idea and rubbed his thighs, which he did whenever he was enthusiastic about something. It was always the first place his pants wore through. He hung the sweater over the back of his chair, then forgot to take it with him, so I had to bike back for it, because he was planning to cook for our friends and still had to swing by the supermarket. I don't remember that bike ride either but I do remember how my brother rode, always at his own tempo, which was so much faster than my own that I exhausted myself trying to keep up with him. He cycled as if he was alone, suddenly veering off into side streets without signalling and weaving between the cars waiting at stoplights. I always followed him furiously, as if he were a fugitive and I was the police. Of course, I didn't have to follow him. My brother never understood my anger. He always thought I should go my own way.

ey Two, my brother said. Look at this.

I stood up and walked over to him. He was standing at his kitchen window, pointing at a boy who was handing out flyers near the park entrance. That's my stalker, said my brother. The boy looked up as if he'd heard my brother speaking and I quickly took a step back but my brother stayed at the window.

He comes to the bar a lot too, he said. I brought him home one night last week and ever since, he's been here, standing on my doorstep.

Why does everyone find bartenders so attractive? I asked. You're literally just a waiter.

He shrugged his muscular shoulders.

Not everyone can do it, he said.

You mean I couldn't do it.

I didn't say that. You said it.

When we first moved to the city and my brother became a bartender, I applied for a job at a Grand Café in the city centre. I worked there for less than a week. On four consecutive evenings, I filled glasses with shaky hands, tapped foamless beers, and attempted to figure out the espresso machine all while pretending I didn't notice how irritated my customers and colleagues were. I thought this was how it was for every beginner but at the end of the week, the manager told me my character simply wasn't suited to the food service industry. It's not just a matter of practical skills, she said. You need to give zero fucks, be untouchable. At the same time, you need to be able to join the fun, put the patrons at ease, play the role. You're too vulnerable, it makes them nervous.

I was shocked by the bluntness of her words.

Welcome to the real world, she said. But the point was that I was no longer welcome to work there. That night I cycled over to my brother's bar, where the lights switched between green, pink and orange. Dressed in a tank top, he made me a strong cocktail without dropping any bottles or asking a colleague which ingredients were needed.

If I can't even do this, I said, then I can't do anything.

My brother deftly lined up four shot glasses in front of a group of young guys and filled them with tequila. He moved back and forth behind the bar at an accelerated pace, grabbing bottles, taking money and winking at customers. It was Saturday, the place was full. His muscles looked good beneath the coloured lights.

Don't worry about it, he said when he came over to my side of the bar to get a cocktail shaker. You'll find something.

He walked away again.

Of course I'll find something! I yelled at his self-righteous back.

And we were both right because a few months later, I started working at the vintage clothing shop.

The guy in front of the park pulled some new flyers out of the pannier on his bike.

What's he handing out? I asked.

Flyers for a festival that's being held here in the park sometime soon.

Maybe that's why he's been hanging around in front of your place and it has nothing to do with you.

My brother sighed.

Maybe, he said. Maybe not.

My brother's short silences were something I only experienced later. Much later, when he was keeping me at a distance and I was thinking about him a lot. I replayed our conversations in my mind all the time and noticed his occasional silences, which usually came after I'd said something unkind. I used to get snappy when I was feeling down but I always assumed he'd tell me if something upset him. And I also thought: Even if you have no one else, you'll always have your brother.

He wanted to go to Hollywood to become an animator for Walt Disney. He filled sketchbooks with cartoon characters and saved up until he had enough money to buy an Amiga computer. He spent entire afternoons on it, creating his own Disney-style animations. But when he didn't get into art school, he just gave up on his dream. No one said to him, *Why don't you just try again next year?* Instead, my mother said, Maybe you should study English like your sister, and I said, Great, now we get to stay together!

I helped him prepare for his admissions interview. What are you hoping to achieve? I asked him. Who inspires you, what is your favourite cartoon character and can you tell us more about Walt Disney? He knew everything about Walt Disney's career and could name every Disney film in chronological order.

When it was time for the actual interview, he hadn't wanted me to go with him and refused to say anything about how it had gone when he returned. It was nothing, was all he would say. After pressing him for a long time, I eventually discovered what they had said. They thought he was technically very good but didn't see enough of his personality reflected in his animations. You know everything about Walt Disney, they said, but who are you?

What a stupid question, I said, after he finally confided in me. We were sitting on the floor in front of the couch. My brother nodded. We agreed it was the stupidest question we'd ever heard. I threw an arm around him and felt him relax.

We had no trouble attracting boys but found it difficult to evade them when they called. Sometimes we covered for each other. I was also unsure of how to let a guy down gently once I was already in his room but having second thoughts. My brother was never around for those moments. There was a boy I met at a party who had hair like Jon Bon Jovi and lived on the outskirts of the city. Neither of his housemates were home. They owned a large TV and a lot of CD racks. I'd wanted to go home to my sweaters. The boy handed me a glass of wine and looked at me with intent. I can't stay long, I said, and thought: *It's too late to back out now.* We did it three times that night and each time it happened, I felt my throat tightening like a screw. I'd left early in the morning. Wearing only his socks and underpants, he walked me to the stairwell, where he kissed me at length, then grinned. I acted all giggly and coy but on my way downstairs, I wished his building would collapse so I could disappear under the rubble.

I was feeding the ducks and beside me a man and a woman were doing the same thing, each with a child. They were chatting about the weather. I didn't know what I should say, the weather was dreary.

When I look at those ducks, all I see are delicious duck legs, said the woman.

Ah, I thought, then said, And look at those geese over there, they're perfect for Christmas.

Well, said the woman, I happen to think geese are ... No, you really can't talk about them like that.

She looked at me, apparently shocked. The man said nothing. The children silently threw the rest of their bread into the water.

Sitting on a bench in the park, I told my brother about the woman who would eat duck but not a goose. I made a little ball out of the empty bread bag.

All my attempts at superficial conversation end awkwardly, I said. I have a gift for broaching painful topics.

When you feed ducks, they start gang-raping each other, said my brother. He'd once read something about male ducks and what they got up to when they were bored.

The other day I was talking to the bike mechanic about the weather, I said. And, naturally, the conversation turned to the children he no longer saw because his ex-wife had moved to Ibiza, where it was always sunny. And then I didn't know what to say.

You have to use clichés, said my brother. It's why they were invented.

For the longest time, I thought that the use of clichés signalled a lack of imagination. I didn't understand they were formulas you could use to keep other people at a safe distance.

Your gift isn't a gift, it's a defect, said my brother. You can't keep your distance.

When I got home, I read on a website for duck enthusiasts that rape was a natural reproductive strategy. For ducks, rape isn't a violent act, an expert had written. Nor is it something they do for lack of a better alternative.

At the bar where my brother worked, a group of friends was quickly formed. We're kind of like family, he said. But I'm your family, I said. He told me they were his queer family and that I had nothing to worry about. As for myself, I was able to form a pair but could never get any further than that. I enjoyed being so naturally present in a friend's life that I'd become almost like a piece of furniture in their house. I needed this to feel like I was a natural presence in the world. Aside from my brother, I've only ever had that feeling with a handful of people. And eventually, it's always ended.

To be a natural presence, you shouldn't take up too much space, which I always found easy at the beginning of a friendship. It felt nice to reshape myself into precisely the right format until the moment came, usually once I'd shrunk to my minimum size, when I got moody. *I always have to be careful what I say around you*, my friends would say. Or if I suddenly lost my temper over something that hadn't previously angered me, they'd say, *I don't have enough space for this*. Then I would know that my presence was no longer a given and it was all my fault — it wasn't fair to pretend I was something other than who I really was, to keep shapeshifting like some sort of Barbapapa. I'm either too much or too little. I'm terrible at dispensing the right dose of myself.

O n Sundays, my brother and I would watch the contestants on the Dutch version of *Survivor* as they attempted to survive on a desert island, doing their best to outperform the others by winning challenges and voting against one another. At first, we watched every episode of every season together, and later, after a few years, we watched them apart. When my brother ended his own life, on May 6, 2016, we were thirty-five years old and had watched fifteen seasons of *Survivor*. By then, only celebrities appeared on the show. The wide-legged stance of the new presenter annoyed me and it took me a while to understand that she probably only assumed that strange position to appear shorter than the man beside her.

When secret alliances between contestants came to light during the first season, great indignation would ensue, from our side too. We believed honesty was the best strategy for survival. However, once we understood how quickly you were out of the game if you refused to lie, we abandoned our principles. *That's the game*, we would say, shrugging our shoulders whenever a headstrong candidate got voted off the island. We didn't make the rules.

In those days, long before I'd met Leo, my brother and I used to discuss our future as if it were a joint project we had yet to begin. I wanted a partner who wasn't competitive and found my presence in his life enriching. My brother laughed loudly at the word enriching. He was hoping for a man with soft hands and an aversion to conflict. They would live in a house on the water. I imagined a small lake with a jetty for him and a shore lined with pine trees in which the man with the soft hands would hang fairy lights in winter. And I wished for snow, thick sheepskin rugs and cable sweaters. I wanted that lake to be in New Hampshire (I'd just read a book by John Irving) and the house would be a lake house we'd share, my brother and I, along with his conflict-averse man and my non-competitive partner. When we weren't in New York, that's where we would be. Usually, we got stuck at this point in the conversation because my brother would say that he liked pine needles well enough but what he actually wanted was a sea with seahorses in it, and did I know that male seahorses incubated their babies? I quickly understood exactly how seahorses mated but I still didn't understand what my brother wanted out of life.

He was lavish with his promises but also believed he was entitled to change his mind. He regularly cancelled appointments at the last minute and when he told me I could borrow his car, he was often out driving it himself. He was generous with his money too. I wasn't jealous but he always had more money than I did and he liked to spend it. I was welcome to borrow whatever I wanted from him. *Take as long as you need to pay it back*, he would say. *There's no rush*. But if I went a while without making a payment, he would send me a reminder. He thought it was a question of responsibility. *You're not my father*, I often told him.

Our father had left us all his savings. We were able to access it once we turned twenty-eight, the age at which he believed people truly became adults. He had children when he was twenty-eight. Neither my brother nor I wanted children. When we turned twenty-eight, we were going to move to New York.

No matter what, I said.

Cross my heart, said my brother.

We celebrated our twenty-eighth birthday at an Italian restaurant with our new lovers. It had been my idea. Over the previous year, my brother and I had been seeing less of each other than usual. I thought it was because he'd started working more nights and was too tired to meet up during the day, which I understood. In the meantime, I'd been seeing Leo for three months but my brother had never met him. And I had no idea who he was spending his free time with. It was Sooyaan, a tall, slender guy in a low-cut shirt that revealed almost all of his smooth, shiny chest. He instantly hit it off with Leo, who was short, broad and hairy.

Isn't it strange that we suddenly know so little about each other's lives, I said to my brother. We're not growing apart, are we?

Even the idea of this sounded so idiotic that I burst into laughter but my brother didn't laugh along with me.

What's the matter, I said.

Nothing. You're always trying to make something out of nothing.

Do you think we're growing apart?

Maybe.

I watched him brace himself.

And maybe that's not such a bad thing, he said. Eventually, we're going to have to lead our own lives.

What do you mean? Why would you say such a thing? My heart thumped. I looked at his boyfriend, who was draping a napkin over his dark blue chinos.

Did he tell you to say that?

According to my brother, Sooyaan had nothing to do with it. Sometimes that's just how things go, he said.

But things don't just happen to go like that, not when it comes to us. My reaction seemed to shock my brother and this made me angry. Maybe he'd assumed that it would bother me as little as it bothered him.

I don't need my own life, I said.

You just don't want to live on your own, said my brother.

But that wasn't it. I did want to live on my own, just with my brother. He said I was easily agitated and he found that difficult.

Difficult, I said. You think I'm difficult.

Madness is like gravity, all it takes is a little push, Leo said to Sooyaan.

They were discussing the new Batman film.

Why didn't you ever tell me any of this, I continued. My voice was shaking. We're still going to New York in October, aren't we?

For weeks I'd been emailing non-stop with our aunt, who had agreed to host us for three months. It would be the test-phase of our move-to-America plan. My brother and I had decided this long ago.

She's going to New York, New York, Sooyaan said. How nice!

My brother looked at his plate and I grabbed my jacket.

We're leaving, I said to Leo.

Outside the restaurant, beside our bikes, I burst into tears. In bed that night, I started crying again while Leo awkwardly stroked my back.

I'm not normally like this, I told him, thinking back to when my mother was always crying and how I hadn't understood what she meant when she said that she didn't have any space for us. This was around the time my father left us and my brother and I were busy conducting geological experiments, throwing heavy fossils from my mother's collection down the stairs, attempting to make the earth tremble.

In the science section of the newspaper, there was an article about an impending tsunami. There would be waves hundreds of metres high caused by a seismic shift on the west coast of La Palma, one of the Canary Islands. The tsunami would completely wipe out Lisbon, Boston and New York. I called my mother and asked her why she'd never told me anything about these impending tsunamis. She laughed. The seismic shift will take at least ten thousand years, she said, and the sides of the mountain in question were likely to crumble gradually, so there will be no tsunami.

It was a weight off my shoulders, my relief derived as much from the news as it was from the way that she told me. I'd rarely heard my mother speak so cheerfully. Maybe it was because we were talking about her area of expertise and I was getting a glimpse of her other life at the Geological Institute, where she was obviously bright and exciting company because the discovery of bones from the Pleistocene was the main topic of conversation, rather than the loss of a family member. I hadn't heard her speak about other men since my father had left us and died, and it made me wonder whether she kept this part of her, just like the cheerful side of her character, hidden away from us. It was as if my field of vision had shifted just a fraction and I was slowly beginning to see something that had existed all that time, just out of frame.

In my apartment on the park, I quickly learned what it meant to be alone. You could buy a pack of salami and eat the whole lot. Or you could eat lunch at 10 o'clock because that was when you happened to be hungry. Maybe I thought too much about food.

We used to bake cakes. We each had our own apron and stool at the kitchen counter. When the cake was ready, we'd present it to our parents and everyone would have a piece. For the rest of the day, the cake would sit on a plate in the kitchen. I'd cut off little slices and eat them when no one was looking. Once, I went too far. My parents noticed how much of the cake was missing. They blamed my brother and sent him to his room and I said nothing to save him. On another occasion, we baked a cake and were allowed to eat the entire thing. We were each given half of the cake, which we put on our nightstands. The following day, my half had gone but my brother's cake was still sitting there a few days later. Whenever he wasn't around, I cut little slices off it.

When he went to live on his own, he became a vegetarian out of solidarity with the animals and environment. He was particularly concerned about global warming. Whenever we argued, I would take it out on the environment by eating loads of salami. But after our twenty-eighth birthday, the age at which a person becomes a real adult, instead of thinking about salami, I pondered the meaning of the word 'worth'. My parents never talked about love. People were either worth the effort or they weren't. I don't know exactly when my brother decided that I was no longer worth the effort. It was only once I realised he'd broken our bond and that there was no ground for me to stand on that

I began to fall. I felt like the coyote in the Roadrunner cartoons my brother and I used to watch, how he would suddenly freeze in the air and look down at the empty space beneath him. Except, my fall wasn't quite as funny. According to Leo, I was very snappy. Luckily, he'd tried to tell me this multiple times, so I was prepared for the Saturday morning when his face flushed with anger and he slammed the door behind him when he left. He stayed away for two weeks and only sent curt responses to my messages in which I explained why I was so snappy (so I wouldn't cry) and why it was good that he was confronting me with my behaviour and making such an effort. I told him that everyone deserves a second chance and that most people were unwilling to change but I would, and I wanted to put in the effort, for him, for us. *Now I truly understand what it means to be alone*, I used to think back then. But I still didn't really understand it at all.

xperiences literally alter the brain, a neuropsychiatrist on TV once said. Every conversation impacts your brain and changes it. Based on the new information, you make different decisions. I'm not exactly sure how long I was falling, how I landed or when I stood up again but I began to walk differently, extra cautiously. Cracks in the ground aren't always visible to the naked eye. Every movement has the potential to take you down.

lza asked if I knew why Leo had come back to me.

I'm very demanding, I said. Maybe he likes that.

She asked if I was selling myself short. She didn't have her notes at hand but was it true that my brother had called me a pessimist just before saying that he wanted to lead his own life?

Not a pessimist, I said. He told me that I was easily agitated.

And does he also think you're demanding?

My whole family does. Because I won't allow myself to be brushed aside when they tell me they're doing fine but they're lying. It makes me angry. Sometimes you have to be demanding because it's the only way to get through to someone.

Sometimes anger can be an expression of sadness, Elza said. And a way to push people away.

But I'm not pushing anyone, I said angrily. They all choose to leave.

osef Mengele showed absolutely no remorse for his crimes in the diaries he kept later in life. He still considered Jews and Romani people unworthy of life. He wrote stories about children and dog stories. This is what his son Rolf told the German weekly, *Bunte*, in 1985, six years after Mengele died.

Contrary to popular belief, Josef Mengele wasn't the only prominent doctor at Auschwitz, as is generally assumed, just one of at least thirty-eight doctors who performed experiments on the people imprisoned at the camp. He hadn't even been the highest-ranking doctor but was the one who worked at Auschwitz the longest and had never asked to be reassigned. Mengele was also one of the few who performed his work without taking stimulants and he regularly volunteered to run the selection process on the platform at Birkenau train station. He stood on that platform at least once a week, smiling as he waited for the transport trains to arrive.

Some of the doctors lived with their families at the camp. Mengele did not. Though his wife, Irene, had come to visit in 1944 and found it idyllic. Earlier that year, his son Rolf was born in Gunzburg. Rolf later became an attorney, specialising in real estate law.

Rolf grew up without his father but had met him twice. Their final meeting took place in Brazil, where Josef was in hiding. His father was planning to commit suicide, Rolf said. He felt that his life was no longer worth anything.

Freitod is the German word for suicide, a free death. Unworthy life is *unwertes Leben*. And a dog story is a story about a dog.

y brother didn't say his first words until he was two. He was sitting in his booster seat in the car, my father had stopped for a red light. *Gween*, said my brother. *Dwive*.

He developed an obsession with traffic. He wasn't particularly interested in cars or motorbikes, it was more about the way people moved through and around each other on the street. The local channel regularly broadcast images of the city set to music. The footage was filmed by someone on a bike and my brother would watch it with bated breath.

Whenever I came to a roundabout, he would make me stop, said my mother. But you always wanted us to keep going because you hated standing still, so there was always someone crying. Perhaps she'd forgotten that my brother had never been the one to cry, because we were always standing still.

I feel so scarce, my brother would say whenever he felt bad but wasn't sure why. My father found this such a beautiful expression that he started using it himself, so frequently that we should have been able to foresee his departure. But even as he was packing his bag, we didn't see it coming. It was only once we were asked to sit on the couch, and he took a seat on the coffee table in front of us and said in a more serious tone than usual that he had to go, and we asked how long he would be gone and he didn't have an answer for us, that it began to sink in.

But why? I kept asking and my father kept saying that he just wanted to be honest with us. My brother kept nervously repeating: Yes, we'd all like that, wouldn't we. And we continued talking in circles until my father stood up, took his bag and disappeared.

It was always dark when I was underwater. Even under the shower, I kept my eyes closed. As a child, I'd take a bath with my brother once a week. If I farted, he'd put his head under the water to observe the bubbles, making it impossible for me to avoid looking at his bottom. When I started to feel embarrassed by my own body, my brother continued to walk around unencumbered by clothes, so I became an unwilling witness to his body as it went through puberty.

Alone in my room, I kept tabs on my own development with a makeup mirror that my mother had got for free when she bought a new mascara. I worried that my left labia was bigger than my right labia. And my left eye sat a little higher than my right eye. In fact, all the features on the left side of my face sat slightly higher than everything on the right. Even my smile was lopsided. But if I looked at a picture of Kate Moss in a Pringle sweater, it was almost as if I grew more beautiful myself. I also found it relaxing to look at colours. Chestnut blended with sea green. Cognac and powdery pink.

After my brother died, I would stare at the sea-green lamp on my wooden nightstand until my eyes grew misty. Or I'd flip through the fabric sample book I'd sneakily taken from the furniture shop on the corner, where my brother had bought his leather couch when we first moved to the city. He saved up and was able to pay for it upfront. Unlike me, he didn't have to go to the thrift shop and buy the least ugly sofa you could get for twenty euros, a worn-out grandma couch in the wrong shade of yellow. Sometimes I would drape a small section of the sofa in the right shade of yellow from the sample book and imagine the entire sofa in that colour. Sometimes I looked at myself in the mirror and imagined my eyes were symmetrical. Or I'd picture my brother beside me, in the same place he always stood when we brushed our teeth as children, him on the left and me on the right, his face always slightly higher than mine.

While we were brushing our teeth, he'd occasionally drop the tube of toothpaste on the ground deliberately and say, Pick it up. He would keep saying it louder and louder until I went to the kitchen to finish brushing my teeth there. When we put on plays, he was always the wicked stepmother and I was the poor orphan. He wore long dresses from my mother's hippie era, and I was always in one of my father's old shirts. Every Sunday morning, we'd perform a version of Cinderella in which I found a new family instead of a prince. A teddy bear stood in for my real mother. This worked well until my brother suddenly decided that he didn't want to do it anymore. I was already dressed in my shirt but he wanted to read a comic.

Come on, I said.

No, he said.

I threw the stepmother's dress at him.

Pick it up, I said.

He walked over to the bookshelf and selected a Donald Duck comic.

Pick it up! I shouted.

No, he said. A no is always stronger than a yes.

He climbed onto a chair and pulled a book off the shelf. It had a naked man and woman on the cover with *Sex Education for Teenagers* written above their heads.

We're not old enough to read that, I said immediately.

My brother flipped through the pages until he came across a photo in which a clothed man was trying to kiss a clothed woman. The man hung over the woman while she struck a defensive pose.

My brother read the title of the chapter aloud. *No Is Always Stronger Than Yes*. But in the photo, yes looked so much stronger.

When I graduated, he gave me a holiday as a present. I was allowed to choose the destination.

Just say the word, he said. The sky's the limit.

I chose New York but he thought that was too expensive, so we ended up on a Greek island.

It doesn't matter to me, I said. As long as there's sun and sand.

It had been raining for months and I was nursing a broken heart. At night, I performed angry monologues in my head, and cried buckets during the day.

My brother said I might have been mistaking my tears for rain because the weather actually wasn't so bad. He laughed loudly, then apologised.

We went to the ugliest, most touristy Greek island but only realised this after arriving. Our apartment complex was on a lane off Bar Street, which had a steady stream of drunk English people moving through it all day. We slept in the basement, and our 'balcony' was just a trench with a wall around it. If you sat there, you could just about peek over the ledge at the outside world. My brother remained optimistic, renting us bikes and ordering me cocktails on Bar Street, but I couldn't stand it. I couldn't stand the sun or the beach, couldn't stand my brother, who liked to walk around naked in our stuffy apartment and, above all, I couldn't stand myself.

I want to die, I said almost every morning and my brother would say it was because of our accommodation. After breakfast, we went to the beach or walked around until we got into an argument. My brother expected me to follow him because that's what I always did. If I wanted to go in a different direction, he would ignore me and keep walking. I'd had enough of it and when I told him so, he said he'd had enough of me. He walked off in the direction of Bar Street and didn't return until the following morning. I was standing in the trench and happened to see him coming down the street.

Yoo-hoo, he called, waving at my head.

He'd met a diving instructor and we were going diving later that day. Another instructor was coming along for me.

Adonis! he cried. Your instructor's name is Adonis!

The four of us sailed out of the harbour.

This isn't a real lesson, said Tom, my brother's Australian diving instructor. It's more of a day out. We're only diving five metres deep.

The wetsuit was stifling and the oxygen tanks were heavy. Their weight could pull me under, far deeper than five metres, where it was cold and dark, where there were fish who never saw daylight, like goblin sharks, also known as living fossils, because they'd existed as a species for more than 125 million years. Or I could sink even deeper, into a chasm formed by colliding tectonic plates, which geologists like my mother called a trough or a depression, but when I looked at schematic diagrams of them, I thought they looked more like inverted skyscrapers, so deep they gave me the chills. The deepest depression was 10,911 metres and had been discovered in 1960, nine years before the moon landing, by two men in a submarine that had barely enough room for two bodies. When one of the outer plexiglass windows cracked during the descent, the sub had started shaking, and the men were forced to endure a panicky 278 minutes before they reached the bottom, where they ate the chocolate bars they'd brought with them.

Even before my head went underwater, I was already sucking furiously on the mouthpiece.

She's a little scared, my brother said to Adonis.

No worries, Adonis said and then made a circle with his thumb and forefinger.

This means okay, he said.

He stuck up his thumb.

This means up.

His thumb turned downward.

And this means down. Now just keep breathing.

I kept breathing so heavily underwater that I quickly emptied my oxygen tank. Adonis offered me his oxygen. He held an extra mouthpiece in front of my face but I shook my head, stuck up my thumb and swam up toward the boat, where I waited for my brother, who was euphoric when he resurfaced a little while later. He could be overwhelmingly happy, that brother of mine.

The following summer, I treated him to a week in Rome because he loved espresso and films about gladiators. Our hotel was good, the weather was perfect, not too warm, not too cold, and my mood was outstanding as we stood next to each other in the Pantheon, right under the oculus, a round eye designed to keep the dome from collapsing in an earthquake, which was something I just happened to know. Together, we stared at the opening in the roof, and I thought about all the other people who had stood there over the centuries and wondered if they'd also been comforted by the perfect symmetry of the coffers in the cupola or the way the light fell straight onto them from the little round piece of heaven above. For a moment, I felt like I was floating under the eye, then I became the eye, looking down at 2000 years of history and all of the nobles, clergy and citizens who had crossed the marble floor beneath the cupola, passing all the petrified saints and tombs in the surrounding alcoves. I pictured my father's face, stony in his coffin, and my mother's equally stony face when she sat at the table, staring outside, and the Valentine's card inside of which I'd written *Love You* to my brother when I'd only just learned to write, and the picture of Jesus I'd drawn beside it because he seemed like such a nice man. The very same Jesus who lifted his face to the heavens and asked why his father had forsaken him.

What do they do with this roof when it rains? my brother asked.

I looked at him sideways, annoyed. He grabbed his map and said that he felt like a coffee. On the way to a café, we got into our classic argument about who would decide our route and he didn't notice when I turned into a side street. Suddenly, I could go wherever I wanted and decided to walk back to our hotel and eat a slice of pizza at the hotel bar. Young men on scooters tooted their horns when I passed by, which never happened when my brother was with me. Meanwhile, I couldn't get my brother's question out of my head. What *did* they do with that roof when it rained?

After Rome, he told our mother that he never wanted to go on holiday with me again. My mother casually shared this with me years later, as if she was talking about two entirely different people.

'd forgotten to go to Times Square, it just hadn't crossed my mind. I'd been circling it for weeks, searching for the perfect winter coat. When I finally found the one, it was too expensive, so I had to wait for it to go on sale. The morning the sale began, I felt antsy. Maybe the coat was already gone. A similar urgency gripped me whenever I walked into a train or restaurant, always afraid that the last seat would be taken right under my nose. Leo can't stand pushy people, the ones who breathe down your neck when they're standing in line behind you, as if shuffling a few centimetres forward would make all the difference. He never wants to be that person. The first time he told me this, we'd only just met and he had yet to learn he was falling for a woman who was like that, perpetually afraid of not fitting in, convinced that there was never enough space for her.

My aunt was a successful real estate agent who sold luxury apartments and owned an enormous loft above a wine bar on Waverly Place. My room faced the street, and I could watch people walking in and out of the bar through the large bay window. I often spotted my aunt among the crowd, and we'd wave at each other. She liked to sit at the bar and on my first evening in the city, she'd taken me down there and tried to set me up with the manager.

I already have someone, Auntie, I said. His name is Leo, you know that.

She did know that but wondered why he hadn't come with me. Because he has to work, I said. And because my brother was supposed to come. She didn't understand how twins could just grow apart.

You were always so sweet together, she said.

Everyone is sweet when they're young, I said.

My aunt said that she thought I was still awfully sweet.

How could anyone ever get tired of this face, she said, softly pinching my cheek.

The winter coat was still available, and there was only one left in my size. Cashmere and almost ankle length. It was made for you, the salesperson said. I walked to Waverly Place wearing my new coat, looking at myself in every store window along the way. It felt as if I was taking a new path in life. Every new coat makes you feel this way.

Just before I left for New York, we'd met on neutral territory, at a sandwich shop neither of us ever patronised. I wanted to know why he'd been keeping me at a distance and he started talking about my meddling, and the time I hadn't allowed him to vote for the Animal Rights party because the party leader was a Seventh Day Adventist.

I still did it, he said. I voted for her and when you found out, you made this face and kept banging on about her worldview and everything that was wrong with it.

We don't believe in the Second Coming of Jesus, I'd said, and maybe I had been a little surly and started a couple of sentences with, *You must*, and, *You can't*, but what he didn't know was that later, after he'd left, I'd come to understand his choice and after I'd thought about it even more, I completely supported it. The Animal Rights party was, after all, a secular organisation, and sometimes it takes people a while to gain that kind of insight.

He said he was happy we were able to rebuild our relationship. A healthy relationship is what he meant, not the unhealthy type that we'd evidently had. I wondered who was sitting across from me — it wasn't the same brother who always had me smell his breath before he went on a date and needed my approval for every tank top he bought, who once said that no one would ever love me as much as he did. But that had been a while ago.

But why didn't you ever say that it bothered you? It was the question I'd been mulling over ever since our birthday dinner. I let him speak, nodding and smiling to show him how much I'd already changed, but once I was home, I realised that I'd never got an answer.

'm single again, he said, when I called him from New York. Sooyaan hadn't wanted to commit and my brother understood that. It was better this way. He was feeling good.

Really? I asked.

He laughed loudly.

Yes, darling.

He never called me darling. Then he said he'd been planning a trip to South America. Sooyaan was supposed to go with him but now he was going alone.

Now? I asked. What do you mean? For how long?

Six months.

He wanted to become a diving instructor in Brazil. He would leave at the beginning of December.

But that's in a month, I said. You'll be gone when I come back.

I just need to be alone for a while, he said. But we'll call and Skype, okay?

You know you can tell me anything, I said.

He told me he had to hang up because he needed to go to the toilet, that he had to go to the bathroom whenever he heard my voice.

I called Elza and told her that I was losing my brother for real this time.

He wants to be alone, I said, in South America. And he won't talk to me and he's acting as if he doesn't miss Sooyaan.

Elza said that contact is something you can't force. He'll either come back on his own or he won't.

What can I do? I asked.

You can cry, she said. It's a grieving process.

I walked from Waverly Place to Ground Zero, counting twenty-six blocks along the way. The construction site was hidden behind skyscrapers. I walked until I couldn't go any further and was able to see the contours of both towers on the ground. When I looked up into the void, the idea of the two towers dizzied me. My brother would have explained exactly what the construction workers were doing underground and what the metal containers were for, even though I knew just as much about it as he did. We'd read the same articles. Still, I would have held my tongue and let him explain everything the construction workers had found when they began building the 9/11 Memorial and the new World Trade Center: a hand, an ear and sometimes entire limbs that had been buried in the sewage shafts for over five years. They'd only stopped searching for human remains a year ago.

On Wall Street, I found a hotdog cart and waited for my turn behind two Italian tourists. When they asked the hotdog vendor about local attractions, he stopped working and started chatting to them. One of the tourists took a map out of his bag and unfolded it. The vendor bent over his cart and ran a chubby finger over the paper. Two open buns lay waiting for their sausages.

Sorry, I said.

All three of them looked at me.

I just wanted to get a hotdog, and then I'll be on my way.

Take it easy, said the vendor, putting his finger back on the map.

I looked up beyond the buildings. The streets were narrow. A body could smash to death on the stones at any moment. It was December 2008, the height of the financial crisis.

Philippe Petit bridged the empty space between the Twin Towers by stringing a tightrope between them and walking across it. Sixty-one metres was the length of the cable he traversed from 2 WTC to 1 WTC. He'd walked back and forth eight times, wearing his black funambulist suit and carrying his black balancing pole.

My brother and I had yet to be born when Philippe walked on a cable 415 metres above ground in 1974. His childhood friend, Jean-Louis, had been involved in the plan from its early stages. Jean-Louis had been careful and critical. He made sure Philippe didn't take any unnecessary risks, so his chance of survival remained as high as possible. The towers themselves were well protected. It was like coordinating an attack, a coup. Everything had to be considered.

My aunt remembered the newsreel footage of Philippe on the cable. She was living with her parents in the Netherlands at the time. Her brother — my father — was already attending university. She didn't want to study. She wanted to do something else, something with money, which is what she used to tell anyone who asked. Her parents' house made her claustrophobic, so she would climb out of her bedroom window to meet her friends on the dike, where they'd drink cheap rum and smoke weed. When she saw Philippe walking across that cable, it was as if she was crossing it herself, high above everyone else. Once he was back on solid ground, Philippe told a journalist what he had been thinking when he first stepped onto the cable. It could mean the end of his life, a feeling he couldn't resist. This is exactly how my aunt felt when she moved to New York without any money and spent her first few months living out of dingy hotels. She said it was dangerous, filthy and overcrowded but there was still more space for her than there had been at home. She told me she'd met Philippe Petit at a party more than thirty years later, when the towers were no longer there, and she'd let him know what he meant to her, and he'd put his hand on her lower back and attempted to stick his fingers under her waistband. She showed me how he'd done it, and I squealed. We'd just watched *Man on a Wire*, the documentary in which Philippe and his friends explain the preparation and execution of their coup, then we'd gone to the wine bar under her apartment because she found other bars too dangerous at night, which was her way of saying that she didn't want to walk the streets when she was drunk.

That's what fame does to you, she said.

I thought about Jean-Louis and the way he cried in the documentary. He'd used a bow and arrow to shoot the cable from the north tower to the south tower. He was the one to make that first connection. They spent the entire night testing the cable and when dawn finally broke, Philippe stepped onto it. He tested his friend's cable, checking it was tight enough. Jean-Louis watched him nervously and when he saw Philippe's face relax, he thought, It's okay. This is how he explained it. And then he cried because he could still feel the euphoria of that moment, the walk on a tightrope 415 metres high, how he and his friend had made it all happen. A project spanning years, in which they were always on the same track, and now all that tension was leaving him. But the grief that followed remained with him too, the loss of his best friend who no longer needed him, who was embarking on a life in the spotlight as if it were a new project that required the same amount of blind determination. According to Leo, natural law dictates that there's always one person who loves more than the other.

My aunt was at Elton John's open-air concert in 1980. My brother and I were only four weeks old at the time. She sent us a picture of Elton John in a Donald Duck suit sitting at a white grand piano. *How wonderful life is when you're in the world*, she'd written on the back of it. Ten years later, my brother found the photo in the bottom of a drawer and hung it on the wall above his bed. I'd wanted the photo too and we fought over it but my brother won because he loved Donald Duck more than I did, and now that I think of it, he probably loved Elton John more too. We never listened to his music, except the song that my aunt had quoted on the back of the photo and that number he did with George Michael but that was released a few years later.

While we were taking our final exams, I bought a Donald Duck costume for my brother. He wore it to our graduation ceremony and to all the after parties. From now on, he cried, I can do whatever I want! He said that from then on, he would only wear Disney costumes but after a few weeks he started wearing his grey sweatpants again. I think the Donald Duck costume is still in a sealed box in my mother's basement. I remember how much we'd struggled to cram that thing into the box.

Someone said that Donald Duck was embroiled in a divorce scandal. I was eleven and lying in my favourite place by the window when I lifted my head from the carpet to look at the TV. Two blonde people, a man and a woman, were grinning doggedly at the camera. Donald Trump, I understood then, was a millionaire who had his own tower. Even the air around it belonged to him, bought with money that was his, not his wife's.

While standing beside the waterfall inside the pink atrium at Trump Tower, I googled Ivana Trump and her husband, Rossano Rubicondi. They'd just got married and were already on their way to breaking up. On the reality show *L'Isola dei famosi*, the Italian version of *Survivor*, Rossano had started something with the supermodel Belén Rodríguez. The water splashed down the marble wall beside me and I thought about newborn babies and how safe the sound of rushing water makes them feel because it reminds them of the womb, the constant rushing of blood. Then I thought about Ivana and everything that was being said about her, that she'd received two hundred and fifty thousand dollars from Donald for each child she bore him and how hard she'd fought for her money when they divorced. You have to fight back, Donald said in interviews, otherwise no one respects you. He saw winning as the most important character trait. Not everyone knew how to win. (Lots of people come close to winning, he said, but then they don't. Because they don't know how to win.) His younger brother, Robert, also didn't know how to win. He had managed real estate outside Manhattan for the Trump Organization and then retired. As a child, he'd given Donald all his blocks, so that his brother could build towers. And Donald had glued the blocks together so that he wouldn't have to give them back to Robert. Donald is proud of this when he talks about it in interviews. He kept all the blocks. He had won. After the divorce, he continued living in the penthouse at Trump Tower, which had been decorated by Ivana and featured a big fountain, marble walls and plush beige carpets, much thicker than the carpet I'd lounged on in my youth. Suddenly, I missed that carpet and my sweaters. Beside me, the waterfall was gushing so loudly that I had to put on my headphones to drown out the sound, so only a comforting rush could be heard.

My aunt named her new poodle Ponzi. She'd come up with the name on the way to a kennel in upstate New York after we heard the news of Bernie Madoff's arrest on the radio. Her ex-husband had worked as a broker for Madoff but as far as she knew, he'd never been involved in any Ponzi schemes. Their marriage had lasted five years. By then, they'd been divorced for over twenty-five years. She always looked after herself, even during her marriage, when her husband had started abusing drugs. You should never rely on others, she once said. It only leads to trouble. Now, she said she was ready for some tenderness in her life. Aside from this, poodles were intelligent dogs and they didn't shed. On the way to the kennel, she attempted to explain what it is the brokers on Wall Street actually do but I only came to understand why they took so many drugs.

My husband was also epileptic, said my aunt, so there was always a lot of drama in our house.

In the months after Bernie's arrest, we followed the news and all the speculation surrounding it. We found Bernie's wife, Ruth, particularly fascinating. My aunt didn't believe that she hadn't known anything about the fraud for all those years. But I did. I understood how you could feel so unimportant that you could only live vicariously through someone else. And when you're sitting too close to someone, you're incapable of seeing them clearly.

Ruth said in a 2011 *New York Times* interview that she and Bernie had attempted suicide together, when she felt they no longer had anything to lose. By that point, she was seventy and Bernie had done three years of his 150-year prison sentence. I don't remember whose idea it was, Ruth said, but on Christmas Eve in 2008, we took an overdose of sleeping pills. While awaiting his trial, Bernie had been under house arrest and was wearing an ankle monitor. Together, they had figured out the number of pills they needed to take. Ruth said she was glad when she woke up the next morning. She wasn't sure how she felt about Bernie waking up. She thought it might have been easier without him. Even so, she refused to leave him after his arrest.

She said that her marriage had been very pleasant most of the time. It was *fun*. Their vacations with the children had been *fun*. It didn't bother her that her youngest son, Andrew, remembered some of these things differently. She'd found it traumatic when her sons had left home to attend university. To add insult to injury, her son Mark had adopted a dog in his senior year. Bernie is allergic to dogs, Ruth said. And Mark was well aware of that.

She'd met Bernie when she was thirteen, married him at eighteen, and worked like a dog to support him through law school. She could have had her own career. And she could have had more conversations with Bernie about his infidelities. But whenever she brought it up, he denied everything. After her sons reported their father, she'd stayed in regular contact with Mark. At least until he also attempted suicide. He begged me to cut ties with Bernie, she said. Both sons felt that she couldn't stay with a man who had ruined the lives of his own family and friends. But she'd seen him as a human being who was suffering, someone she'd loved her whole life. When Mark took his own life in 2010, she said he was a devoted father who had chosen to abandon his children. By then, she was no longer visiting Bernie in jail. Her failure to listen to her son was something she'd regret until her dying day. She'd do better by Andrew. Then Andrew died from a rare form of cancer a few years later.

I emailed my aunt the interview. That woman is lying, she answered, it's the only possible explanation. She also wondered why Mark hadn't adopted a poodle all those years ago. Poodles are hypoallergenic, everyone knows that.

On the same evening that Ruth and Bernie Madoff had been counting out their sleeping pills, my aunt and I were eating three different kinds of cheese at the wine bar below her apartment. Ponzi was lying on my aunt's lap. He would turn and lick her face every now and then, which she cheerfully permitted. My aunt said she was lucky that she still had enough work during the economic crisis. She also told me about the final year of her marriage, when my uncle had started sleeping at the office because he tended to work late and start early. They only saw each other on Sunday afternoons, when they would have lunch together at the restaurant opposite his office. He never noticed when she made an effort with her appearance. One evening, he returned home. I can't do this anymore, he said. For three whole days, she watched his mouth, observing the way it changed shape when he cried, a shape she'd never seen before, one that didn't suit him. On the third day, she packed her bags and moved into an empty apartment that she happened to have the keys for because she was an apprentice real estate agent. This was before she started working for herself, so she had to sneak around. She moved from apartment to apartment for several weeks until she'd found an affordable studio on the Lower East Side.

There were a lot of empty warehouses there in the 1980s, she said. I didn't have a lot because I was just starting out but I built a life for myself. This apartment — she pointed upstairs — has been paid off, I can retire in five years if I want to. And I never asked my ex-husband for anything. Nor my parents.

I thought about the money my father had left me. I'd been able to access it the previous summer. It was twenty thousand euros, so quitting work wasn't an option for me. Besides, I'd recently got a raise. Just before the financial crisis hit, my boss had promoted me to manager and head buyer of her clothing shop. You've made yourself indispensable, she said, and I blushed. At the same time, my brother had risen to manager of the bar, a promotion that hadn't seemed to surprise him. The economy had sunk into a depression but we were making progress.

Tell a lie loud enough and long enough, Adolf Hitler said, and the people will eventually believe it.

I had three days left in New York before I would head back to my apartment on the park and Leo, whom I missed terribly. I had yet to learn that after three weeks in Brazil, my brother had decided to push his return from June to December. He would be gone an entire year, which I would only discover once I was finished googling.

I googled Trump and the Twin Towers, read about the radio interview that Donald Trump had given a few hours after the attack in 2001, in which he said that he now owned the tallest building in downtown Manhattan. Trump has tried to build the tallest tower in the world three times but each attempt has failed, though he's never put it that way himself. If you say that you're the best in the world often enough, people will eventually believe it, said Donald, who kept a book of Hitler's speeches on his nightstand. He wouldn't admit to owning the book but Ivana had confirmed it, as had the friend who'd given it to him.

I'd read enough and was just about to close my laptop when an email from my brother appeared onscreen. He was happy, he wrote. He hadn't had his first diving lesson but he'd been surfing and met some interesting people. He wasn't the only person searching for themself in Brazil. There were plenty of them! He was surfing a lot in the ocean and surfing very little online, and he laughed — haha — at his own joke. It might take some time for him to respond to my messages. He sent me kisses with lots of exclamation marks, as if he was trying to convince me of something.

My brother wants to discover who he is, I said, as my aunt entered the room with a Chinese takeaway container in each hand.

That's great, she said, letting her handbag, which was dangling from her pinky, drop onto the table.

t's going to be fine, my boss kept saying, but the year that I didn't see my brother, her business went bankrupt. I was given thirty sweaters when I was let go. Leo watched me stack them neatly on the windowsill, as if our window was a shop display. There are some men's sweaters as well, I said. But he said, If you add any more to this collection, I think I'm out. I didn't understand exactly what he meant by this but I did understand that what is comforting to one person can stifle another.

That night in bed, I tried to look at my sweaters through Leo's eyes. The pale light of the streetlamps drained them of colour, turning them into a thick wall of grey wool that I could touch if I stretched far enough. I threw off the duvet and walked through the living room to the balcony, wanting to feel fresh air against my skin.

Out of habit, I tried to identify my brother's apartment on the other side of the park. Naturally, none of the lights were on because he was currently on the other side of the ocean. When we used to walk to school, we were careful never to let a lamppost come between us, or our bond would be broken and we would have to go back and pass it again, both of us walking on the same side. I don't remember the day my brother started that particular game but I do recall the day he suddenly stopped playing it.

The next day, I shared my decision with Leo. I was going to set up an online sweater shop to sell part of my collection. Of all the new sweaters I bought each year, I would keep only a few for myself.

Sweater, I said proudly. That's the name of my shop.

And I wouldn't need anyone else to help me execute my plan.

called my brother in Brazil but he didn't answer. Later he sent me a text: *Happy Birthday!!!!* Again with all the exclamation marks. We'd just turned twenty-nine. Leo gave me a wooden vulva.

It's a prototype, he said. I'm still in the experimental phase.

In his spare time, he'd been making small wood carvings. The decorative vulva was perfectly asymmetrical, with large, ornate labia and folds crafted with the same degree of precision as the wooden statues of saints that stood above the choir stalls in the gothic church in Ulm, not far from the family house in southern Germany where Leo had often spent his holidays as a child. The church had a tower that was 16,153 metres tall, the tallest church tower in the world, which I'd read on Wikipedia before we visited it. As we walked under the three enormous, pointed arches at the entrance, Leo said, Gothic arches represent the vulva. The first gothic churches adopted the form from pagan architecture without knowing that the form referenced the vulva. What? asked his mother, who had been walking right behind us in her turquoise Crocs. Pointed arches, said Leo, are vulvas. Vaginas. His voice echoed through the enormous space. Where does it say that? his mother whispered. She studied the folder that she'd taken from a rack by the entrance.

We hung our vulva above our front door, next to the wooden Jesus figurine that Leo had found in a garbage bin. Almost all our friends wanted one, so Leo made more vulvas and sold them in a Dutch design store. It hadn't made us rich but it did make us enough money to buy new front teeth for Leo after he tripped over a stray sheet of metal that happened to be lying around. The new teeth were whiter than the others, so he promptly bleached the rest. I did the same, and everyone who saw us together said that we were glowing but this was also because we were happy.

eo's Christmas box contained ornaments and a nativity scene with wooden figurines that his grandfather had carved. His great-grandparents had been woodworkers from southern Germany, who moved to South Holland to make clogs at the beginning of the twentieth century. His grandparents were also woodworkers, and their son, Leo's father, initially learned their trade but had gone on to become a consultant at an insurance company.

A week before our first Christmas together, Leo retrieved the box from the attic. My family used to do this too, he said.

I don't believe in family anymore, I said.

But I thought the figurines were beautiful. Leo put them underneath the Christmas tree that we'd struggled to haul up all the stairs. We had a Christmas box and we celebrated Christmas. I felt excited, like I had been the first time Leo and I went to the garden centre to buy plants for the balcony together. Finally, we were real people.

One dark December evening, I looked out the window and saw Leo turn into the street on his bike. I watched as he leant his bike against the façade of our building and searched for his keys in the pockets of his work overalls. Routine activities, as if it was nothing special that he actively chose every day to return to this apartment, to me. The downstairs neighbour's Christmas lights gave him a red aura. It's a miracle, I thought. With his keys in hand, Leo looked up. When he saw me standing there, his eyebrows shot up in surprise, as if I was the miracle.

Whenever I couldn't sleep, I'd think about our tiny apartment and how Leo and I would divide it if we stopped loving one another. Affordable places in the city aren't easy to find. Maybe I could live in the bedroom and the living room and replace the bookshelves with a kitchenette, and Leo could have the kitchen and study. Sometimes I'd cuddle up to Leo, throw my arm around his middle and press my cheek against his broad back. I could lie like that for the rest of my life. Leo breathed faster in his sleep than he did when he was awake. A bed and a wardrobe would fit easily in the study. I wasn't sure how we'd deal with the shower and toilet. I could obsess about it for ages.

'm so glad we're rediscovering each other again.

It was only when my brother said this that I understood exactly how long he'd been gone. He had already started the healing process but our estrangement still felt fresh to me.

We sat opposite each other at the kitchen table. He'd just returned from Brazil and his hair was wild. We looked outside. The winter sun was shining weakly.

Maybe I need to be quicker to raise the alarm when something's up with me, he said.

I asked him if he was perhaps seeing a therapist too.

He nodded. Yes, I started seeing one recently. I'm just going to put on something warm, he said and disappeared into his bedroom. When he returned, he was wearing a dark blue zip-neck sweater.

I gave you that for our twenty-first birthday, I said. Do you remember?

Maybe he was thinking about that day, us drinking champagne in the lobby of the most expensive hotel in the city and how important we'd felt in our vintage designer jackets.

He asked how things were going with Leo, and I said things were good and that we were getting married. This shocked him.

But it's not going to happen for a while, I said. Maybe you could say a few words at the wedding.

And he said that he would. He got excited and raked a hand through his hair repeatedly, a gesture that was new to me. It looked rather sweet.

I dreamed that my brother destroyed everything in my apartment. I was lying in bed and heard him raging in the living room. Once it was quiet, I stepped out of bed and went to take a look. All the furniture was tipped over. White stuffing had come out of the sofa cushions. Drawers were hanging out of cupboards, their contents spread across the floor. My brother was standing in the middle of the room. He was cleaning it all up.

At my wedding, my brother said he knew of no one more like him than I was. The crowd had to laugh at that. We had the same brown hair, the same green eyes, and lately, the same radiant teeth. After seeing my teeth, my brother had got his own bleached.

He said it felt good to see me so happy with Leo but he was also slightly concerned about himself and how he would fare without me. She's always been there, he said, even when I didn't want her to be.

Everyone laughed again.

He told our wedding guests about the way I'd followed him around as a kid, how he could never seem to shake me off. I remembered all the times he'd closed his bedroom door behind him and pushed a stool in front of it so that I couldn't get it open, and how I would stand at the door, waiting because I wanted to tell him the latest news about a film I'd just seen or a graze I'd got or the unkind things our mother said to me. Sometimes I threw things at it, soft things — stuffed animals, cushions — things that wouldn't make noise or cause any damage. But he'd stay inside, and I'd stand outside. I wanted the door open. He wanted it closed. I'd keep talking while he stayed silent. We were nothing alike.

He spoke about the only year in our lives we'd gone without seeing each other because I'd been in New York and he was in South America. He was happy to be with his little sister again, with me, because even though I could be too much at times, there was far too little of me when I wasn't around.

I'm afraid you'll have to share her with me, he said to Leo.

He grinned, and Leo grinned back, baring their new teeth at each other.

The same year that Mark Madoff ended his life, my brother moved in with his new boyfriend, Marcel. Marcel was a left-wing politician. He was fifteen years older than my brother and a vegan. My brother also became vegan, just as I turned vegetarian. Marcel watched with amazement each time I loaded up my plate. He only ate small portions himself. My brother also began eating less. Marcel had a slight lisp and my brother had recently started lisping too. This bothered me most of all. Just be yourself, I told my brother, and he would grumble a little.

Marcel and my brother bought two cats and named them Three and Four. Whenever they went on holiday or to a yoga retreat, I would look after Three and Four. I did this regularly. I loved those cats. They were smart, affectionate animals and softer than some of my sweaters. Cats made Leo itch and gave him rashes, so instead of them staying with us, I would go and stay with them. I'd sleep in Marcel's enormous bed, and early in the morning they would come to lie with me and we'd watch the cargo ships passing by on the river. Marcel lived in a modern apartment on the wharf with lots of designer furniture and floor-to-ceiling windows.

That first summer, my brother swam out among all the ships. Marcel and I stood on the wharf, attempting to keep track of his head between the waves. After a short while, I found I could only look at Marcel's tense face.

It's like he's gone crazy, Marcel said.

Let me know when he's safe again, I said. And I also said it was pointless trying to stop him, that my brother couldn't be stopped. Marcel nodded and because I was happy to be sharing my concerns with someone, I added: I don't think it matters to him whether he lives or dies.

Of course it matters, said Marcel. Last night we went out for a beautiful Indian meal together.

He began waving wildly and I turned back to the water. My brother's head had surfaced in the wake of the first ship. He dove under the waves, then reappeared a few metres closer to the shore, closer to us.

Marcel called out to him. Then again but louder. My brother swam on calmly. The second ship was coming closer, maybe there would be just enough time for him to swim around the front of it.

You know he can't hear you, I said.

During his dynamic meditation sessions, my brother was allowed to act as crazy as he wanted. He and Marcel did the meditations together, in the same way that they did everything: with complete dedication. Looking back now, I think only Marcel was truly dedicated, while my brother was just pretending. Maybe that's why it bothered me so much. And probably also because, in order to reinforce our reunion, he'd sent me some YouTube videos in which Osho said things like *only love and its failure can turn you inside*. And, *togetherness will be rich, infinitely rich, if both the persons are utterly independent. If they are dependent on each other, it is not togetherness — it is slavery, it is bondage.*

I sent him a video in return. A clip from an American talk show in which Osho was speaking about his personal secretary, Sheela. *A love affair never ends. It can turn into a hate affair. She did not prove to be a woman, she proved to be a perfect bitch.* The audience laughed loudly at the word bitch.

My brother laughed so much during his Osho period that I found it difficult to interject. Smiling was a way of keeping people out of your head even though you'd opened your head when you parted your lips, Deborah Levy wrote in *Things I Don't Want to Know*. I didn't send that quote to my brother.

Marcel prepared an Ethiopian meal for our thirtieth birthday. He locked Three and Four in the bedroom so Leo could come too. Marcel usually refused to do this. He believed that pet allergies were psychological, an expression of undiagnosed fear. He thought it was good for Leo to be around the cats, so he could get used to them and conquer his fears. My brother didn't say he agreed with Marcel but did say that he understood Marcel's point of view. In recent months, we'd communicated mainly by phone. I wasn't sure if this was because of Marcel, because of Leo or because of who my brother and I had become: two people who no longer looked at one another. His cheerfulness sounded forced but I said nothing about it. He ignored my rigid attitude and didn't ask how I was spending my time.

Marcel wore an apron over his cardigan, and my brother had on a bright red shirt that appeared new and made him look pale. He apologised for the state of his belly. He said he'd stopped doing yoga and needed to fast and get moving again. I said that taking a break might be good for him. He went silent for a moment, then started speaking eagerly about a sweat lodge ceremony he was looking forward to, the following week in the Belgian Ardennes. It was a gift from Marcel, he said. The less I said, the happier he sounded. I won't allow myself to be criticised by you, he seemed to be saying but perhaps it was best not to attach too much meaning to his tone. Sometimes people sound happy because they are happy, Leo would say later, once we were back home and I had put my brother's birthday present next to the plunger in the cupboard under the sink.

Instead of giving me earrings, like he usually did, he'd got me a ceramic Tibetan neti pot, a kind of watering can used to clean out your nostrils. It's a miracle cure for colds, he said. He was very impressed by that thing. He'd given up tissues for good.

Marcel nodded earnestly. I thought about the boxes of tissues on the nightstand beside their bed.

Thank you, I said. Maybe Leo can use it for his allergies.

It's designer, Marcel said to Leo.

I ran a finger over the mandala etched into the smooth porcelain. I'd once seen something similar displayed in the window of a gift shop.

As I did every year, I gave my brother a sweater, this time a striped Breton.

Lovely, he said and held the sweater away from him as if it was a cat that wanted to take a swipe at him.

We talked about food, pets, yoga and holidays. Leo suggested the four of us take a trip to his family's German cottage in September. I watched my brother closely. He nodded slowly. His face looked doughy and grey.

We just booked something, he said. But perhaps another time.

He walked into the kitchen carrying the empty plates, and I followed him. What's the real reason you don't want to go on holiday with us?

He put the empty plates in the sink and turned on the tap. He said that he wasn't sure it was a good idea. He said something about too many opposing energies in one room and I smacked the bench with the palm of my hand. Two forks clattered to the floor.

I don't understand any of this, I said.

He said he found that a pity. He said this very calmly, as though he'd rehearsed it. But when I said he'd been brainwashed, he lost his patience and slammed one of the sophisticated kitchen cupboard doors shut.

There he was again. My brother. I put my arm around his shoulder to calm him but he shook me off and walked into the bedroom. When I bent to pick up the forks, I felt a cat rubbing against my legs. Leo, who had just entered the kitchen, immediately turned back around. I called out to him, Keep on walking and get our coats because we're leaving now, then we left, and this time, I didn't cry.

Sometimes we fought about our memories. Which memory belonged to whom? In any case, I was sure it had been me, not my brother, who had driven our mother's car through the neighbour's hedge and that I was the one who won a medal at the school marbles tournament. Extensive research has shown that twins are more likely to claim each other's memories. And yet, they tend not to ascribe their own memories to each other. This is why I found it strange when my brother insisted it was me who had swallowed our mother's last three sleeping pills in one gulp at fourteen, when I am certain it was him. He'd slept through the night and right through the following day, and I had to ride all the way to school on my own.

We met Jasper when we were sixteen. He was new to our class and lived in the city, close to our high school. One of his parents was a doctor and the other was an engineer. His left ear was pierced. I'd learned that if you had your left ear pierced, it meant you were gay.

That's such a typically provincial misconception, said Jasper. He liked to call me provincial.

Suddenly, we were three. Jasper often rode with us to the village after school because, according to him, it was no fun at his house but it was clear that we weren't to ask him about that. Once we were home, it wouldn't take long for Jasper and my brother to lock themselves in his room.

This went on for a couple of weeks until one afternoon when the three of us found ourselves sitting on the sofa together: Jasper, my brother and me.

It's about time you learned how to French kiss, my brother said to me. If you wait too long, it'll never happen.

He'd recently become an expert in this field too.

I learned how to French kiss ages ago, I lied, shocking myself.

Who did you kiss then, they both asked. Who.

Someone you don't know, I said.

That's impossible, said my brother. I know everyone you know.

You don't know everything, I said. And to Jasper, My brother thinks that he knows everything.

Yeah, said my brother. I know everything, I'm number one and she's number two.

Jasper giggled, then said to me, I'd like to kiss you. He leaned towards me. The giggling stopped. I tried to push him off but he grabbed my wrists with one of his hands and lay on top of me, his face hanging right over mine.

Mouth open number two, he said. I'm going to teach you something. He squeezed my breast with his other hand, then pressed his hips into mine. It reminded me of the time my brother had put me in a headlock and I hadn't been able to move my arms or legs. All of a sudden, we weren't playing anymore and when that happened, a fit of rage had boiled up inside me, catching me by surprise.

Mouth open, Jasper repeated.

I spat in his face. Jasper rolled off me and went to sit on the floor, using his sleeve to dry his cheek.

Bitch, he said.

Fuck off, said my brother in response.

Why didn't you do anything? I asked once Jasper had left.

Sorry, he said.

After that, it was just the two of us again. He's an asshole, my brother would say every time Jasper's name was mentioned, and a feeling that it was somehow my fault would creep over me.

There was a man who worked on the park maintenance crew named Little Miepie who reminded me a bit of my brother. He was much taller than me. I'd always greet him when I walked through the park, which was almost every day. From time to time, he would attempt to engage me in conversation, and to shield us both from my awkwardness, I'd keep it brief. Still, he kept on trying. It wasn't as if he found me particularly interesting — I quickly realised that he tried it with everyone. Once I understood that he didn't expect any substantial contribution from my side, that he only needed to get some things off his chest, I regularly indulged him. He told me that trees of the same species don't compete with one another, that despite what most people think, they actually coordinate the growth of their branches and keep each other alive through a network of roots. He was also sure that Johan Cruyff would have made an excellent prime minister because he understood how to get people to work as a team. He only needed me to nod along or ask him open questions. The rules were clear. If I accidentally broke them by sharing some of my own knowledge or telling him something about myself, he would say *yeahiknow* and power up the leaf blower to signal that it was time for me to move on.

We were eleven and driving with our aunt back to her hometown. She'd returned from New York the previous day. She asked if we'd ever seen a dead body. You mean a corpse, my brother clarified, then said that he had. The oldest man in our town had died the previous year. He'd been ninety-four, born in the nineteenth century, long before televisions were invented. My brother and I occasionally did his shopping, at our mother's request. He loved tinned green beans and full-cream quark. During the Second World War, he'd gone into hiding and afterwards had become a xenophobe. His petition was the reason there was no centre for asylum seekers in our town. My brother and I hadn't known this when we'd asked him how to put an end to all the wars in the world. We suspected he'd lived long enough to have an opinion on that. He answered that as far as he was concerned, all the bush people who lived in the desert should just wipe each other out. This was shocking to me, because if the oldest person I knew understood even less about the world than I did, then how was it possible that other adults had all the answers? And what was the point of living longer if you weren't going to get any wiser? Even my brother didn't have an answer for that.

The neighbourhood bade him farewell one Friday afternoon between three and five o'clock. He looked like he was going to a party, dressed in a corduroy suit with his thin hair neatly slicked back. My brother reached out and touched his hair when no one was watching. Now you do it, he said but I was too scared.

My aunt pulled into the driveway of her parents' house and said once more that we should prepare ourselves because our father might not look like himself, which is why I hadn't counted on the corpse having the same nose and lips as my father, and the same tiny bump above his left eyebrow that I always ran my finger over when I sat on his lap. He also looked like he was going to a party. But his hair wasn't slicked back, it was combed to the side and instead of touching him, my brother kept his hands deep inside his pockets, fists visibly clenched.

Leo and I had bought new curtains, and that's what I was talking about when my brother shared his news. We were standing at his front door, and I had borrowed his stepladder to hang the curtains. They were light grey felt and I'd thought they were beautiful when I bought them but now, I was afraid the colour was too sombre.

It was the lightest grey they had, I said, but maybe I should have gone for a warm oatmeal colour instead.

I want to leave Marcel, said my brother. But I don't know how to tell him. And I don't want to abandon the cats.

Shock brought a lump to my throat. I wasn't used to this kind of openness from him. For several years, I'd had to settle for superficial contact and I'd stopped asking him any tough questions. Like whether he meant what he said at my wedding, that he missed me when I wasn't around. Maybe I hadn't missed him during the past few years either, when he'd been completely preoccupied with finding himself. Leo and I were doing well. But it still felt like I was waiting. He'll come back on his own, Elza had said. Or not, she'd added, but I only remembered that part much later.

If you're living together and have cats, I said, you can't just get up and leave. You have to fight for your relationship.

He said that while doing various types of therapy, he'd come to understand that he wasn't attached to life. Even as a child, he wasn't bothered by the thought of dying. If you're dead, you're not missing out on anything anyway. He wasn't particularly attached to his presence in the world, or the presence of others either.

I put the stepladder on the floor between us and peered over the top rung at my brother's face. His eyes were always open wide, as if he was in a constant state of bewilderment. It was amusing to watch him read a funny book or step in the spit of one of the men who frequented the Turkish coffee house downstairs, especially if he was wearing his slippers. But now he was squinting at the sun and his top lip was curled up, like a rabbit. I'd always wanted to tell him how this looked.

I'm scared of pain, he said, but I'm fine with death itself.

Fine was the word he would use when I asked for a bite of his sandwich, if I wanted to borrow his stepladder or one of the neighbours happened to throw a loud party. Almost immediately, he'd got to know nearly all the residents living on Marcel's side of the wharf and he always knew exactly what to say when he ran into them. *Uncomplicated* was the word people used to describe him.

I said that I didn't like what he was doing. That it wasn't enough, he had to commit, he owed it to Marcel and the cats.

Wow, you're being difficult again, he said.

The waiter recommended we try the steak tartare. We don't eat meat, I wanted to say but my brother said: Bring it on. He also made hand gestures, as if he had no time to lose. Lately, he was always in a hurry, just as I was feeling like standing still. The roles had been reversed. The steak tartare was served with wafer-thin toast and a poached egg. I stuck my knife into the egg, my brother ate around it. He ate all the meat and left the rest.

On the way to the restaurant, I'd prepared for our conversation. I'm worried about you, I intended to say. I miss you.

The last time he confided in me, there had been a stepladder between us, and he'd caught me a little off guard. A month had passed. Our new curtains were beautiful. The colour wasn't too sombre. I'm busy, my brother kept saying whenever I reached out. If I just keep on trying, I thought. Waiting to see what would happen no longer seemed wise. My brother needed someone.

So, I said, I think it's a shame our interactions are always so volatile.

Yes, said my brother. And that I left Marcel without giving it another try.

No, I said. Yes, maybe that too.

I can never get it right with you, said my brother. Why are you always so pushy?

I'm trying to reach out to you, I said. Hello!

Hello, said my brother. Here I am.

He closed his eyes to concentrate on tasting the meat. An overhead light was shining a warm beam directly onto his forehead. He looked as though he could ascend at any moment.

ver since having a panic attack on the highway, my brother had refused to drive. He'd stopped in the emergency lane and called me. I had to come and get him. How? I asked. I didn't have a car. He said he couldn't breathe and I told him to tilt the car seat back and try to breathe slowly. Inhaling for four seconds and exhaling for six, just as he'd learned at yoga. I counted out loud for him. I said that he wasn't going to die, that he was only anxious and anxiety always passed (unless it didn't but I left that part out). Eventually, he would be able to drive home slowly, like a geriatric, in the right lane, behind a semi-trailer, it didn't matter. Now you have a good excuse for not being the fastest, I said. You'll see how much this will relax you. His voice sounded normal again when he said he'd do whatever it took to make sure he was the absolute slowest. He drove to my place, parked in front of my door and walked through the park to his own house, where he and the cats were living again. From that day forward, the car was mine, on the condition that I was prepared to chauffeur him whenever he needed to leave the city.

One day, I drove him to the beach. We put our jackets in the sand and lay down on them. It was still too cold to lie there like that but I hadn't wanted to change position. I closed my eyes and listened to the rushing of the sea. My brother cleared his throat.

What is your greatest dream? he said.

I said I still dreamed of a life in New York, of Leo and me in a brownstone on Prospect Park with steps leading up to the front door and my brother living in another brownstone on the other side of the park.

Do you know how big that park is, he said, and how much those houses cost.

I asked what he dreamed about.

For a long time, I didn't have any dreams, he said, because if your dreams don't come true, you're stuck with them.

And now?

Now I dream of disappearing.

What do you mean, like Dad when he left?

No, truly disappearing.

Like Dad when he died?

He said: I don't want to die but I don't want to live either.

I said: If you truly disappear, that means you can't come back.

Contemplating the finite nature of everything didn't cause me to panic and I was able to take the metro without checking everywhere for bombs but I did break into a sweat whenever I ran into a vague acquaintance at the supermarket or if I got a phone call from an unknown number.

In the park, on my way to see my brother, I listened to a radio interview with an artist who made films about islands. She quoted John Donne, who'd said *No man is an island* and emphasised how important it is to feel like part of society, rather than an island. Everyone is afraid, she said. Some people are scared by what they read in the newspaper and try to change the world. Some retreat into their cocoon and avoid connecting. And this makes them feel less involved in their environment, they're less engaged.

The fight or flight response, I thought. I'm afraid it's why I don't worry too much about climate change. Still, I have managed to make a few connections. Leo, for example. We'd been living together for five years. You're shutting yourself off, Elza said recently. You're not talking to him about what really concerns you. You're avoiding intimacy. No, I thought, my brother does that. People often get us mixed up.

Rather than speaking about himself, my brother preferred to talk about deforestation in the Amazon, films or supermarkets. Leo also liked to talk about supermarkets. He'd scan the leaflets for discounts and then shop at several different supermarkets in one morning. He almost always returned in a bad mood because Albert Heijn was out of rocket, or there hadn't been enough space to move around the aisles at Dirk van den Broek, or the manager at Lidl had once again been regaling the shelf-stackers with stories about his private life at the top of his voice. But if I volunteered to do the shopping, he'd say: No, that's not what I want, I like doing it.

My brother was standing in his kitchen, slicing vegetables. I went and sat on the windowsill.

Do you know what anxious laughter is?

Naturally, he knew what it was. Using laughter to express fear, he said. Or discomfort.

But it's also using laughter to disarm. Diminishing yourself so that you don't frighten others.

He asked which self-help book had taught me that. I laughed and said I'd just been doing some googling and he started hacking away at a spring onion.

One of the artist's films about islands featured a volcano that had lain dormant for several hundred years. Nobody knew when it would reawaken. Entire families allowed themselves to be photographed in front of that mountain, while something that could cause an eruption at any moment was boiling away inside it.

There are people who hire themselves out to stand in queues for other people. I was looking for a second job because I wasn't making enough money from my sweaters.

That doesn't sound like it would suit you, said Leo. You'd get burnt out immediately. Once you start earning enough, you'll be the one hiring people to stand in queues for you.

I'd never thought about it like that. I had considered mindfulness, sitting still and breathing. Since my brother's panic attack, I'd been thinking about breathing a lot. If I could just keep breathing, him too, especially him. And Leo, of course. Leo and his leather crotch. He'd bought black and bright blue bike shorts with a matching shirt. That kind of clothing doesn't come in pastel colours. He felt he needed to work on his body. We fought about his bike. He wanted to hang it in the living room, above the sofa, because there wasn't enough room for it in the stairwell. We never argued but a bike on my wall was too much for me. Suddenly, it's your wall, said Leo. He was standing in front of the TV in his cycling outfit, looking up at the empty space on the wall above the sofa. I said I found it visually offensive, a bike on the wall.

The outfit is cute, though, because you're wearing it.

But Leo couldn't be sweet-talked. He said that his racing bike had to be kept dry and if the bike couldn't go on the wall, then he didn't want my sweaters next to the bed. I said I didn't see what my sweaters had to do with it. They were part of a collection, which was steadily shrinking and even earned us a modest income and if it bothered him, he should find somewhere else to sleep. Leo slept beside me that night while his racing bike stood upright in the meter cupboard. He took it out three times a week. When he eventually quit cycling, we used the handlebars as a shelf for our stacks of toilet paper.

My brother said he was broken and couldn't be repaired. He was lying on his sofa.

You're not perfect, I said. But that's not the same as being broken. He closed his eyes and shook his head softly but did seem reassured for a moment.

You have to keep taking your pills, I said.

He nodded.

My sickness is what he called his depression. If I asked him to come over for dinner, he'd say he couldn't because of his sickness. Or if I made a joke, he'd say, I can't laugh at your joke because of my sickness. Is your sickness coming too? I would ask when we were arranging to get together (dropping in unannounced hadn't been an option for quite some time).

I stood up and opened the curtains. We can commemorate the dead at home or go to the war monument in the park, it's your choice. He chose to stay home but we went to the park because I felt he needed to spend more time in the company of others. Besides, it occurred to me that he'd been the one to choose the previous year.

A large crowd had gathered at the monument. Parents lifted their children onto their shoulders so they could see the speakers. We were standing behind those people and couldn't see a thing. A child's voice read a poem. A toddler sitting on her father's shoulders in front of us farted audibly. I looked over at my brother, who was looking at the ground.

Come on, I said. We're leaving.

We were heading back to his house through the park when

the two-minute silence began. But we were already silent, so it didn't count. As my brother stood still, I realised that standing still was also a way to commemorate the dead and, in that way, we were able to do something for those who had died. I refused to think about my father because he hadn't been a victim of war. I wondered if my brother was thinking about our first corpse, the old neighbour from our village. I also thought about Auschwitz and Josef Mengele's twins — I'd been googling a lot that day — and then the two minutes were up.

Mengele was particularly interested in firstborn twins, I said. Did you know that?

My brother kicked an empty beer can towards a bin. The eldest is always destroyed first, he said.

looked up the article about Mengele's interests again and realised that I'd misread it: he hadn't been particularly interested in *all* the firstborn twins in the camp, he'd been particularly interested in Tibor Offer, or Tibi, which is what his younger brother, Miklos, called him. Tibi and Miki, prisoners 5103 and 5104. Miki said during an interview that Mengele was always singling out Tibi because he was the eldest.

The eldest always gets more attention, is what he must have thought, even in a concentration camp.

Tibi endured four surgeries without anaesthesia. He became paralysed after an operation on his spinal column. During a subsequent procedure, his genitals were removed. After the fourth operation, Miki never saw his brother again.

Why do you keep going on about Mengele? my brother said one day. I'd just finished telling him about the Bavarian farm where Mengele worked as a farmhand when he went into hiding after the war. His work had mainly consisted of sorting potatoes. The largest potatoes were for human consumption, and he'd throw these through the trap door on the left. The middle-sized potatoes were to be replanted, and they went through the middle trap door. And the smallest ones went through the window on the right, into the pit used for pig food.

You're not even Jewish, my brother said. You're not an identical twin. You're not a victim of anything.

I was ashamed of the hours I'd lost searching for stories of Holocaust survivors and the way I used the great suffering of others to process my minor grievances. I was allowed to cry about the

Holocaust. My brother didn't seem to notice my embarrassment. I'm your blind spot, I often said to him and then he'd say he was mine.

I cried for Miki, for all the family he'd lost in the war. After the war, he married a woman who died giving birth to their daughter. He remarried and had more children but he never got over losing Tibi. It's impossible to find the words for it, Miki said about the day that his twin brother disappeared.

Tibi and Miki were the youngest of four sons. They grew up among the fruit trees on the land owned by their parents, who made liqueur from the fruit. Josef Mengele was the oldest of three sons. His parents had a factory that produced agricultural machinery. At home, they called him Beppo.

Miki found celebratory moments most difficult. The people he preferred to share those moments with were no longer around. Beppo resented his German family for not sending him cards on his birthday. Both of them complained about sleeplessness, nightmares and loneliness. Miki hit his wife and kids. Beppo was abrasive, critical and domineering, especially when it came to his son, Rolf. Two women left him and he outlived both his brothers. The death of his younger brother, Lobo, affected him most of all. They were estranged because Beppo was quite intense and short-tempered. It was only on Lobo's deathbed that Beppo attempted to repair the relationship. He sent Lobo a letter but received no response.

When Miki discovered that his brother was still alive in 2005, he was already seventy-four years old. After the war, Tibi had ended up in Ukraine, while Miki had settled in Israel. The Cold War had made searching impossible and perhaps it didn't even occur to them because each of the twins was so certain that the other was dead. *Wait for Me*, a Russian television programme that found missing people, reunited them after sixty years apart. The website of the American Holocaust Museum dedicated a few lines to their story but I couldn't find any more information about their reunion, not even the episode of the TV programme, and after an entire day of futile googling, it seemed as though I'd imagined it.

Elza's father had survived Auschwitz and her mother, Bergen-Belsen. Her father believed that Bergen-Belsen can't have been as terrible as Auschwitz. Both Elza's parents felt that people who hadn't experienced the concentration camps had no reason to complain. They met each other when they were twenty, shortly after liberation. Elza arrived a year later. To keep myself from complaining, I tried not to feel anything at all, she said. That worked for a while, until it didn't. She said this during an interview with an online psychology magazine about the hierarchy of suffering. (According to Elza there is no hierarchy of suffering.) I'd been in therapy with her for a few years when I read the interview. In the meantime, her grandchildren had started school, and my brother had yet to die.

Oh yes, said Elza when I brought up the interview. That was quite some time ago.

Can I ask you something?

Yes, of course.

I carefully asked about her parents, her childhood. Her father sold slippers to hotels and had travelled often. Her mother was a calm and distant woman. She taught her daughter to look after herself as early as possible. At five, Elza was already taking the tram to school alone. She'd been fond of asking questions as a child. Why is the sea salty? Where do your ears end? Why don't I have a grandpa and grandma? But if she ever crossed the line, her mother would start to scream.

I could never be sure which of my questions would cross the line, she said.

Their family lived on the third floor of a block of flats in a blue-collar neighbourhood in the city and they had an allotment in a community garden where Elza would play in the mud, and her mother would sit at her easel. The fact that she painted was unusual in their milieu.

She painted branches and leaves, said Elza. Only ever branches and leaves.

I asked Elza if she found my questions annoying. You try your best to understand people, just as I do. It's not your fault your family can't handle that.

I'm not Jewish, I said. And my parents weren't traumatised by the war. I'm not a victim of anything.

For the second time in my life, I was using my brother's computer without his permission. It had been three days since we'd last heard from him and Leo was calling hospitals. After a few attempts, I guessed the password for his laptop — UncleDonald2.0 — and was just starting to read through his emails when he walked in. I expected him to yell and pre-emptively flinched but instead, he collapsed onto the sofa beside me and started to cry. He'd taken the train to De Hoge Veluwe National Park. Impulsively, he'd booked a room in a hotel and invited someone from a dating app to join him but when his date knocked on the door, he kept quiet until the man left. After that, he remained in bed crying for two days.

And now I'm doing it again, he said.

He was curled up on the sofa, lying with his head on my lap. His enormous feet hung over the edge of the sofa, as if they belonged to someone else. For the first time, I noticed how small he was.

Come now, I said.

There wasn't much else I could say. I took him in my arms and rocked him like a baby. When he fell asleep, I sat there, still as I could. Outside, the sky turned pink then gradually darkened. I thought about all the love we have inside us and how only a shred of that reaches the people we care about.

'm with you, I told my brother when he panicked at night. I'm here. There were moments I wasn't entirely there and would think about the laundry I'd left in the washing machine or which window could be opened so that I could get some air. Hold on to me, I told him repeatedly. I don't know if I said this for myself or for him.

If I could just stay close enough, then my brother couldn't leave. He gave me shopping lists and I bought coriander, coconut milk and lemongrass for a Thai curry that needed to taste the same as the curry he once had at a vegan restaurant he'd been to with Marcel. He never spoke about Marcel anymore but did talk about that curry. He'd never tasted anything quite so delicious. But the chef wouldn't reveal the recipe. It was a family secret and she said it would remain so. Since then, my brother had been experimenting with curries but his creations didn't taste the same. Maybe it wasn't the curry that had made the evening unforgettable, I suggested every so often. And maybe you shouldn't attempt to unravel the mystery. Maybe, he'd say. Or maybe it just needs some more lime zest.

When he wasn't busy perfecting his curry recipe, he worried about bombings and refugee boats capsizing and the computer cable he'd ordered but hadn't received, fretting so much that he had to take something to calm himself. He wondered what had happened with the order, whether the cable was in stock, if he'd entered the address incorrectly or the packet was lost. It was a cable used to connect his phone to the TV. There were days he was sure it would never arrive. And days he suspected the neighbours had intercepted it, or he'd get the feeling that it could be delivered at any moment and would therefore refuse to leave the house.

For the longest time, I didn't realise it was anxiety that I was feeling, said my brother. I thought that everyone felt that way, that it was normal to get heart palpitations at the sound of the tram.

I only realised how distressed I'd been once the distress was gone, after my brother drowned himself.

Elza said: It's good to rationalise things but sometimes it can be just as good not to rationalise and instead consider how you feel. I asked her why she said this. I was in a bad mood. Where does it come from, she asked, your bad mood. I said that I didn't know but of course I knew.

On one side of the park, there's Leo, I said. On the other side there's my brother. And I walk back and forth between them with bags full of groceries.

Leo and I had taken time off work to go to Germany for two weeks but when the moment came, I didn't want to leave my brother alone, so we stayed at home. Or Leo stayed home and I walked back and forth.

He could clear out his workshop, I said. He's been planning to do that for a while. There are woodchips all over the floor and lately, he's been saying that it really bothers him. But instead of doing that, he's just lying on the sofa drinking beer all day because he says he's on holiday.

At least my brother still had active days when he'd take boxes of old computer hardware and comic books downstairs and dump them on the street. He was also busy dumping his old friends. If they called, he wouldn't pick up the phone and if someone rang the doorbell, he'd cautiously get off the sofa and hide behind it, as if the unexpected visitors could see him up there on the second floor of the building. I'm seeing fewer people at the moment, I heard him say to a friend we happened to run into in front of his building one day. The friend held a string attached to a giant balloon with GET WELL SOON printed on it. The friend worked at the bar.

My brother had been on sick leave for quite some time.

Oh, said the friend. He handed the balloon to my brother.

I have to go to the supermarket, said my brother. I'm out of cat food.

(This was true, I was forcing him to go because I felt he needed some fresh air.)

The friend nodded.

I'll go on ahead then, my brother said to me and walked away from us with GET WELL SOON bobbing merrily in the wind above his head.

Screaming can be such a relief, Leo said to my brother. And if you don't want to worry your neighbours, you can always scream into a cushion.

That's what he did too. I watched from the windowsill as Leo looked around for a cushion but there weren't any in my brother's kitchen. My brother asked Leo when he was most likely to scream into a cushion.

When I'm home alone, he said. That's when I feel most free.

Then you must have been doing a lot of screaming lately, said my brother.

Leo looked up.

It'll lighten your load, he said.

Can I ask you something? I asked. Which cushion do you usually scream into?

Turns out it was the colourful Moroccan cushion that Leo always put under his head when he took a nap on the sofa. In fact, it was a cushion he hadn't wanted because he didn't like the colours but eventually, he'd allowed me to buy it on the condition that he could put the giant copper frog he'd bought at a flea market in the corner of the living room. I pictured him screaming into a cushion he hadn't wanted, with the copper frog as his only witness.

For a time, my brother would only eat bananas. There were peels all over his house. I was forced to eat the pasta that I cooked for him alone and the stress always made me eat too much. Still, it was my brother who put on weight, not me.

Leo said he was willing to come over and cook occasionally but I wanted it to be like it used to be, just my brother and I, at home alone. But apart from this, nothing was the same. My brother slept a lot during the day and at night I would have to hold his head to calm him down. In my opinion, people don't support each other's heads anywhere near enough. Except for my aunt, who always held my head firmly in her hands when she greeted me by kissing both cheeks. The head is one of the most vulnerable parts of our body. During a fight it should always be protected.

The brain isn't as good at putting things in perspective at night, I told my brother. His head was in my lap and I was massaging his temples.

How do you know that.

I read it somewhere.

It's not getting any better, he said then.

You're depressed, I said. You really can get better again.

But I'm not sick.

Suddenly, he no longer considered himself sick.

He screamed. When you want to die, everyone acts as though you're sick. Why isn't life the thing that's sick? And all the people who wish to die perfectly sane?

Some people are listened to, and some people aren't. I had heard one of the judges from a talent search show on TV say this earlier that evening. You're already a great singer, she said to the contestant in front of her, but you also have to have something to say. Say it unapologetically. Say it with your soul. People need a reason to keep listening.

I like watching talent competitions. Rather than watching the contestants, I always look at the contestant's family members, watching the way they absorb every second of the performance as if they were the one standing up there singing, getting so emotional that they forget themselves and cry. It's empathy, its mirror neurons, it's emotional contagion, my brother would say. Pigs can do it too.

Generally, I walked away when my brother started ranting but that night, I looked at his reddening face, which was still lying in my lap, and listened to what it had to say.

The folders on our desktop were named Plan A and Plan B. Plan A was life and Plan B was death. I was in favour of Plan A, my brother leaned towards Plan B but changed his mind daily. I followed his lead. I listened. Sometimes we worked on a safety strategy designed to prevent him from accessing lethal substances but there were other days when we'd sit side by side googling which powders to use for a painless death. We worked diligently and methodically, eating handfuls of those jelly beans you can buy in party-size bags at the supermarket.

When he said that the worst of it was behind him, he was looking over my head at the view outside. It was one of the first sunny mornings of the year. The window was open and the rose-ringed parakeets in the tree opposite his place were screeching. Some of the neighbours complained about the parakeets, claiming that their nests and noise took up too much space. But my brother felt we should have thought of that before allowing them into our country. The parakeet droppings would turn the pavement beneath the tree white and he would scrub it away a few times a year.

Hey, he called out of the window at a tourist emptying her pockets into a basket attached to a bike. That's not a garbage bin!

I'm going to start exercising again, he told me.

He was wearing running shoes for the first time in months.

And I'm going for Plan A. We can throw Plan B out the window.

He gestured casually at the open window, as if it was nothing.

I was sitting on the sofa with a book when my mother called. Leo was at the supermarket.

Your brother's gone, she said. He took the folding bike and left a note.

I asked what she meant.

He's gone, my mother repeated.

He'd also left a map — a Google Maps satellite photo with an 'X' marked at the spot where the river forked, where the water was widest and deepest. That's where she sent the police.

The second time she called to tell me they were dredging the river. And the third time she said: He's dead.

I stood at the window, looking at the houses on the other side of the park. I'm always afraid you'll get mad at me, he'd recently confessed. His voice had sounded calm, unhurried. And I'd been so relieved, happy to connect with him again, however briefly.

The bike path beside the river was narrow. If another rider was approaching from the opposite direction, one of the two would have to turn onto the grass. The first to swerve was the loser. The narrowness of the path upset my brother. He thought it should be made one-way. Actually, he thought it already was, and never moved aside for anyone but after encountering a man who'd also refused to deviate from the path, my brother had written a letter to the city council. After receiving no response, he'd written another letter. He enclosed photos of the bike path and the swollen knee and scraped chin he'd sustained from the collision. The city council responded with sympathy but also wrote that the path could not be made one-way, so my brother took a plank of wood, cut it into the shape of a stop sign, painted it red and fastened it to a tree at the end of the path so cyclists wouldn't ride onto it from that direction. A few months later, the sign suddenly disappeared but up until then, my brother had been significantly less bothered by oncoming traffic, at least that's what he told us after each subsequent ride. I don't know how it had been during his final ride.

When I cycled over there, the bike path was cordoned off with tape on both sides but you could easily crawl underneath it. I leant my bike against a tree at the top of the hill and walked down to the water, crossing the wide tire tracks left by the fire engine. I found an elastic hairband by my feet at the shore. It might have belonged to one of the rescue workers who had dredged up my brother and his bike. The water was calm. Three swans were swimming further upstream and a cow was standing on the opposite bank. My brother had often sat here on the waterside. We sat there together sometimes and he'd shown me how to whistle on a blade of grass. Three short, three long, three short — SOS signals. I knew that the water close to shore was almost waist high. But only a few metres in, it got too deep to stand. I tried to peer through the water's murky surface, as though it were possible to see what had happened beneath it but I could only see myself. Crouching down, I let my hand sink into the water. It felt chilly, summer had yet to arrive. I scooped up some water with my hand and took a sip. Wanting to taste the last thing my brother had tasted.

Someone once said if you soften your eyes, it would make you relax and drop your mask. It was a woman with small eyes who said this, I could barely see them in the short film I found bookmarked in my brother's browser. The woman said that softening your eyes helped you see yourself and everyone around you in another light, a better light. *Compassion* was the word she used. My brother had also used that word for a while, back when he was still meditating and reading Chinese philosophers. He had compassion for all the abusers, dictators and meat-eaters in the world. He even had compassion for Bernie Madoff, our father and Josef Mengele. I understand, he said, where the impulse to harm another comes from. I feel it too. I didn't ask him where his own impulse came from or why he found it necessary to go away without me. He'd recently returned from Brazil, and I wanted to be a better sister to him, someone uncomplicated, someone with compassion for others and very little compassion for herself. Part of having compassion for others is having compassion for yourself, said my brother with a certainty that annoyed me. People who harm others also have the capacity to harm themselves, I thought.

I tried to soften my eyes while thinking about the day that my brother rode his bike into the water. I'd spoken with him on the phone the night before it happened. We'd talked about his feet. They'd grown, at least half a size, and he suspected it was because of the antidepressants but there was nothing about larger feet mentioned in the list of side effects. I said that women's feet grew during pregnancy and menopause due to hormonal changes but he was neither pregnant nor menopausal. He said he couldn't do anything about that, he was only stating the facts. I said his belly was bigger than it used to be and that his larger feet might be the result of his weight gain. He said he had to hang up. It was something he often did in the middle of a conversation, always just as I had the feeling that we were on a roll.

was standing at a stoplight wearing my running clothes. Rather embarrassingly, I was running on the spot, with my sweaty face hidden under a cap. A truck was speeding towards me. And I thought, What if I just ... Now. NOW. Then the truck passed, and the opportunity was lost. My brother had gone and with him, all of my past. I came from nothing and was going nowhere.

After learning of his death, a song kept getting stuck in my head. It was the same song we played at the funeral. My brother would often sing it in the kitchen while stirring risotto in the large cast-iron pot he'd bought from a luxury kitchenware shop for a few hundred euros. We ate risotto at least once a week. And I would sit in my usual spot on the windowsill and sing along. When the window was open in the summer, I would scream the words at the outside world, at the parakeets in the tree opposite his house. People passing by would glance up or shout something in response but I felt untouchable. I was sitting high, I had a brother, I had a voice.

I didn't picture my brother singing the song, I only thought about the words and heard the melody playing over and over again. It kept me from sleeping. If you're having trouble sleeping, it's best to stay away from your phone, and avoid external stimuli. But I was overstimulated from within, I had to find a way to drown out the broken record in my mind. So, I'd listen to an American podcast and the murmuring voices would send me to sleep. But every musical intermezzo woke me up and the music in my head would begin again.

Sometimes I went to my brother's house in the middle of the night and crawled into bed, so that I could relax without keeping Leo awake. I'd smell a jar of my brother's hair wax that I hadn't thrown away and it was wonderful external stimulation because I'd suddenly find myself next to him on the sofa, brushing the knots out of his hair — we had the same curls but his were always messy — and I'd feel the thing in my chest trying to force its way out. It would also make the music in my head disappear for a while.

My doctor asked which song it was.

Ween, I said. Help Me Scrape the Mucus off My Brain.

She didn't know the song, so I sang a few lines for her. It was a plaintive but catchy, country-tinged song about spending the dog food money but your man loving you just the same and telling your baby that if they really loved you, they'd help you scrape the mucus off your brain.

After that, there's an instrumental bit, I said. I'm not very good at singing that part.

My doctor asked if something was causing me stress.

What does it look like to you, I said. Ever since the song had got stuck in my head, there was no space for pleasantries.

My doctor smiled. She thought I was joking.

Humour is a biological response to fear, I said.

You mean psychological, said my brother. A psychological response to fear.

He spoke the way he always did when he knew better: quick, confident, happy.

When the song finally left my head, it created space for recurring thoughts. The way my brother would say *you're paying top dollar* whenever he thought something was too expensive, and how after a certain moment in time (Which moment exactly? What had I done?), he stopped calling me whenever he was going to do something fun, how he'd asked me if his face was too shiny and then taken a paper towel out of his pocket to blot his forehead. I also thought about the word q u a r t e t and the way my brother would say it when he had one, so emphatically that I began to hate playing quartets. And the word q u a r t e r, how beautifully he rolled the final r in that word.

specially for me, Leo bought tickets for *Camp*, a theatre performance about the Holocaust featuring miniature puppets in a miniature version of Auschwitz-Birkenau. The puppets were led into miniature gas chambers and their miniature bodies were pushed into miniature ovens, body after body. The show lasted for about an hour and there was no dialogue, just rhythmic mechanical sounds.

Afterwards, Leo and I sat silently opposite each other in a café. Our chairs forced us to sit with our backs straight, looking at one another. I gazed past Leo at the bar.

Don't look, I said. But here come Merel and Romy.

Leo stared at the coaster on the table in front of him.

Have they gone yet? he asked after a minute.

No, they just arrived.

Should we leave?

Merel and Romy were our downstairs neighbours. They'd moved in six months earlier. Merel's parents had bought the entire building as an investment in their daughter's future. Merel and her girlfriend occupied the ground level and first floor. The second floor was being renovated and was going to be rented out for a fortune. The third floor was ours. I had no interest in meeting new people or befriending anyone who hadn't known my brother but Merel and Romy kept asking us to come over for a nice cup of coffee and each time we went they would share some news about the house. They were going to install a roof terrace right above us. Then they asked if we would mind keeping the hallways and stairwell clear and free of our belongings. The last time we'd been there they told us they were also planning to renovate our apartment. You'll have to move out temporarily, Merel had said. But once it was done, we'd be able to move back in. Except the rent would be a little higher. Merel was a few years younger than us. She spoke quickly and cheerfully, as if nothing was wrong. The rent was going to be raised by five hundred euros.

We can't afford that, I said.

Hmmm, said Merel. Are you guys registered with a social housing association?

Leo started fidgeting in his chair. You have to wait at least twenty years to get a decent house through them, he said.

Gosh, yeah, said Merel.

Leo suddenly stood up.

Do you know how difficult it is to live in this city if you don't have rich parents? he yelled. Do you understand that you're throwing us out onto the street? We'll be homeless! We'll have to sleep in the park!

Calm down, said Romy. It's going to be okay.

We'll shit on your doorstep every day!

I shook my head in horror.

I will! Leo said. I'll shit on your doorstep every single day!

And then we'd gone back upstairs.

Of course, we could have moved into my brother's apartment but it turned out that we also had the right to refuse the renovation. So that's what we did, we wrote an email. It's a shame it has to be like this, Merel and Romy replied. I was pleased. There were no more coffee dates.

I'm not leaving, I said. I just got here. Relax, we'll ignore them. They're just two tiny puppets in a café full of tiny puppets.

In a city full of tiny puppets, I thought, in a country full of tiny puppets, in a world ... etcetera. At least one of the puppets had recently lost her brother but that brother had also been just a puppet on a bike. Among all the other puppets riding their tiny bikes in the countryside. Most of the puppets had kept on riding along the bike paths but this one had gone — splash! — into the river. While another puppet — with the same brown hair and eyes as the other puppet — had simply been sitting at home, in the city, in her tiny apartment on the park.

L eo was sleeping on the sofa with the television switched on. There were three empty beer bottles on the floor. He woke up when I reached for the bottles.

What's the time? he asked.

Late, I said.

He asked if I was going to sleep at home or at my brother's apartment again. I said at home. I'd already spent the entire day sitting among my brother's things. We'd cleared out most of the smaller stuff but the furniture was still there. The sofa with a dent in the place where he always sat, the cabinet his keys had scratched. I'd left his sweaters in the bedroom. There were seventeen of them, one for each of the birthdays we'd shared since moving to the city.

That day I sat on the sofa, not in the dent, and read through one of his notebooks, number three of fifteen. He'd numbered them all neatly. While pouring myself a glass of water in the kitchen I spotted his favourite mug in a cupboard, the one with the moustache on it. I smashed it to pieces on the tiles under which he'd only recently had radiant heating installed. Who would install radiant heating if they wanted to die?

The notebooks were in a drawer in his desk. I didn't have to search for long. He'd told me that he was keeping a diary on the advice of his therapist but the writing wasn't helping him. I read number fifteen first. It contained primarily short, factual accounts of each day. Got up at nine o'clock, he'd written, after another sleepless night. I'm leaving today.

He had gone to the village to help our mother with her garden. He often did this if he was feeling well enough. The day before he died, he'd ridden to the hardware shop to buy a new overflow ring for our mother's drain. They had three different kinds and he bought the wrong size. So he had to go back to the shop. Our mother had offered to drive him but he wanted to go on the bike. He questioned her driving skills. Her technique on winding roads is appalling, he wrote. These were the last words in his notebook.

scanned his notebooks in search of my name. He usually referred to me as Two, sometimes just T.

Two can cook quite well when she wants to.

T. knows I want to die and she's putting on a brave face. She can never find out that I've already tried.

He shouldn't have left his diaries in a drawer if I wasn't supposed to know this. For someone who knew everything, my brother could be incredibly stupid.

He'd got in his car and taken the road to the beach. It was a winding road where everyone drove too fast and there were lots of fatal accidents, particularly at night. He'd driven there in broad daylight, even though he hardly dared to drive, but he had to do it for the very last time. Right before a turn he put his foot on the accelerator and then, only then, realised that by spinning off the road he'd be putting other drivers at risk. In the middle of the turn, he'd taken his foot off the accelerator and used all his strength to correct his steering. He only just managed to do it. At the next intersection he turned around and drove back home. No heart palpitations, relieved.

My brother believed that all misery began with hope. Or maybe not all misery, he said, but certainly a lot of it. You shouldn't believe that things will get better. As a child you have to make do with what you have, parents who are never around and a sister who is always there, whining.

It was the summer before our last year of high school. Our mother was on a hiking trip. My brother was sitting next to me on the sofa, rolling a joint.

But I don't whine, I said.

He sighed and switched on the television.

In his YouTube history I found a 1970s film about the Bhagwhan's ashram in Poona. It ran for one and a half hours and for the entire duration I focussed on random snapshots, images without context in which people roared with laughter, screamed, wept plaintively, removed their red robes and rolled their bodies into balls. Why did my brother think that this was beautiful while my whining wasn't?

I looked at a photo of Sheela, who'd led the Bhagwhan's commune in Oregon at the beginning of the 80s and fled to Germany when she was under investigation for criminal activities. The photo was taken the moment she was arrested, just as she was being handcuffed and taken away with her assistant Puja, who was also known as sister Mengele because, among other things, she'd deliberately given 750 Oregon residents salmonella poisoning. Sheela and Puja were both grinning.

The laptop was heating up on my lap, so I grabbed a comic book from the cupboard to put underneath it. *Spike and Suzy: The Threatening Thingamajig*, a complicated story about a thingamajig and a time machine.

Homosexuals should be given their own habitat, said Osho in a speech that was posted online. They could live there happily but they shouldn't be let into our society, where they could spread all kinds of dangerous diseases. *Divide the world into a heterosexual section and a homosexual section and let there be no communication between them.*

I f you were to examine all the telephone bills I received between my eighteenth and twenty-eighth birthdays and add up all the nightly phone calls to and from my brother, you would arrive at 318 hours and 36 minutes.

Elza asked how I'd come up with that number and if I'd really taken the time to calculate it.

Leo kept asking with increasing frequency whether I would be sleeping at home or not. He tried to keep it light-hearted.

It's not a problem, he said, if you want to spend the night at your brother's place.

Because I'm tired and I sleep better over there, I'd say. Because the roof is leaking and I have to be there in the morning to let in the repairman anyway. Because we have to use the apartment, otherwise we can't justify the rent.

My mother paid the rent but never stayed there. I began to enjoy the mornings, having coffee at the kitchen table, my bare feet on the warm floor. Sometimes I wore his clothes and made scrambled eggs, moodily stirring them in his cast-iron frying pan. Other days I spent lying in his bed because it was too painful for me to stand up. I had stomach pain. My brother had a lot of stomach pain in the weeks before he died. He said he had stomach cancer but refused to go to the hospital because that meant dying a slow death.

You don't have cancer, I kept saying. You're not going to die.

At first, I thought I could feel what he felt, that it was a form of phantom pain, and this did me a world of good. But then I started thinking about cancer and called the doctor.

You don't have cancer, she said.

She asked me if I could look after myself. Of course I could do that. If only I'd been able to look after my brother. That was something I hadn't been able to do.

Among all the grey paving stones in our village you would occasionally come across one that was bright blue. We walked past at least three every day. You'll die if you step on them, my brother always said. One day he deliberately stepped on one of the blue stones. You're going to die! I yelled. Not on a Friday, he said. Fridays don't count. My brother invented rules to scare me and then used others to put me at ease.

He once told me something he'd experienced during his childhood. *His* childhood, not ours. He and six other boys were sitting at a long table in Lars' living room. Lars was turning nine and they were all having cake. His mother warned the children that the carpet had just been professionally cleaned. My brother had never seen a carpet that had been professionally cleaned, our parents only ever vacuumed our carpets. He gave Lars his birthday present, a comic book. Lars tore off the wrapping paper. Sjef van Oekel? he asked. Yes, said my brother. He found the scene in the piano store particularly funny. Lars opened the book to see Sjef van Oekel stumbling upon two people having sex in the bushes. Ew! he shrieked. The other boys stood around him and giggled. This is disgusting, said Lars and threw the comic book onto the clean carpet. His mother snatched it up, flipped through it, shot a look at my brother and then put it on top of the bookshelf.

After the cake they went to a playground. My brother followed the other boys. First down the tunnel slide, then over the obstacle course, and then to the jungle gym, where he got stranded because the other boys abruptly ran over to the seesaw and sat on it, three on each side. No space for you! Lars yelled at my brother. And the others laughed. They seesawed slowly up and down, shrieking every time their feet touched the ground. My brother stood by the jungle gym with his hand wrapped around the cold steel and shit his pants. It just slipped out. He tied his jacket around his waist and left it there for the rest of the afternoon. They ate hot chips. Lars' mum asked if he was as crazy about football as the rest of them. He was driven home along with two of the other boys. The boys whispered to each other, snickering softly. Lars sat in the front seat pinching his nose. Don't do that, his mother said.

And when you came home, I asked, what happened then?

You were on the swing in the garden, said my brother. You were the only one home. I remember this because I was calling out to Mama very loudly and you yelled back, loudly, that she wasn't home. When you came inside, I ran into my room and pushed a chair in front of the door. You stood at the door whining for a bit and when you finally backed off, I was able to go to the bathroom and wash myself.

He sat beside me on the sofa. I put my hand on his leg, looked at it, then withdrew it.

How awful, I said. Why didn't you say anything? And why did you think you had to deal with it alone?

My thirty-sixth birthday was spent at my brother's apartment. Leo was allowed to join me if he came empty-handed. No presents, no cake. According to the Meteorological Office we were experiencing an ozone episode. Anyone who went outside would walk straight into the smog.

I swept some breadcrumbs off the floor and found a Spike and Suzy comic underneath the sofa. *The Threatening Thingamajig*. I picked it up and put it back on the shelf. There was always a threatening thingamajig. Maybe it was time to give away the rest of his comics.

Through the window, I watched children playing in the park. A girl and two boys were sitting on the grass underneath a tree. I guessed they were around thirteen. The girl was wearing something that fashionistas would call a playsuit or a romper. The boys wore wide, baggy shorts and had their shirts wrapped around their heads like bandanas. They took turns wrestling with the girl, rolling over each other, and when one of the boys would stop and lie still, tangled up with the girl, the other boy would intervene and the rolling around would begin again. The boys would only roll around with the girl, not with each other. I tried to see which of the boys she preferred, most likely the smaller of the two, the one with black hair, because she laughed loudest with him. I saw Leo walk past the kids, his empty hands in his pockets. It was warm outside, he looked tired but he shuffled along in his flip-flops, straight through the smog, to get to me. According to the Meteorological Office, excessive physical activity should be avoided. I considered waving at him but didn't.

You should never put a gay man in a closet, I said to my mother.

She kept the framed photo of my brother that had sat on his coffin during the funeral in her closet. I took the photo out of the closet and put it on the bookshelf. Exactly one year had passed since I'd last seen him, three days before he died. He had smelled like sweat, he needed to wash his clothes more often but I no longer found it necessary to tell him that kind of thing. He still did his laundry at my place. Come to visit me more often, was the only thing I said to him. And don't forget to bring your laundry. I sounded like the mother of a son who'd recently come of age but nothing like our mother.

She was sitting on the couch and I was in an armchair. The television was on with the sound switched off and we were talking about cuddles.

You never cuddled me, I said.

I did cuddle you, she said. I cuddled you all the time!

The fact that I sat on her lap so often as a child was entirely due to me. I kept a close watch on her lap and climbed onto it whenever I had the chance. She'd allow me to sit there but she didn't cuddle me. Not actively.

Actively cuddling someone means that you actually put your own arms around the other person, I explained.

I cuddled you, she said again.

I remembered how I would lay my head on her chest and wrap her arms around me while she watched television or talked to my father. Sometimes I'd fall asleep.

148

The love between parent and child is like every love affair, I said, repeating what Elza had told me earlier that week. In the beginning it's very physical. Then it becomes verbal, more detached. As children grow more autonomous, they become much less a part of you.

Maybe I found it difficult, said my mother. Gradually losing the two of you. At least I wasn't forcing myself on you. I thought: if something is wrong, they'll come to me. She looked over at her son on the bookshelf. One day you'll be old and our relationship will become physical again, I said. But I won't be the one wiping your bum.

I was using a tea towel to dust miniature porcelain cups before lining them up neatly on the windowsill. They belonged to the toy tea set that my brother and I used to play with. My mother had brought over the tea set on her way to the hospital, where she was having a melanoma removed.

Calm down, she said. It's just a little spot.

And then she was gone.

I'd just put down the fourth cup when I saw something move out of the corner of my eye. An enormous man was standing in the park. His head was hovering over an elm tree and he was staring straight through the window. I froze and thought about my brother, and then the man blinked. It was a giant puppet wearing what looked like an old-fashioned diving suit without the helmet. A French theatre group was doing a street performance, I'd read about it in the newspaper. The man and I were still looking at one another. He wasn't blinking anymore, and neither was I. And I thought: I won't be the first. Then he started moving again. An industrial crane was holding him upright and there were cables attached to his arms and legs and all these little men in red suits — gnomes — were pulling the cables with all their might, working very hard, with someone screaming directions at them through a megaphone. The giant walked slowly away from me, through the park, towards my brother's house.

My brother was the giant and I was a gnome. I was all the gnomes. I was way too much. And still, I hadn't been enough.

ook at your legs, said Elza, and then think: these are my legs. What nice legs.

I tried it, looking at my legs. They used to be slim. It was good that my pants were covering them, that I wasn't sitting there naked. My pants were made of brown silk. When I lay my hand on them, the bright red plaster around my thumb looked good against the brown of the pants. Elza asked what I was thinking.

I'm thinking about the colour red in combination with brown, I said, looking at Elza's lower legs. They were perhaps a little too pale but certainly more elegant than mine.

My brother had beautiful legs, I said. They were muscly but lean. And rock hard. Even when he put on weight, his legs were still beautiful.

And what do you think of your own?

They work, I said. They're not broken. They're not a pile of ash in an urn.

Exactly, said Elza. She sounded elated. And your stomach works, and your arms, your back and your feet. Try to be happy with the body that you have.

I nodded and said: I'll try it this week.

y eyelids were starting to droop. I examined them in the bathroom mirror and wondered whether my brother's eyelids would have got droopy if he had lived. Yes, I decided, looking at myself with disdain. Leo came into the bathroom, wearing only underpants. He'd developed tiny boobs. I tried to squeeze his left boob but he pushed my hand away.

I have a terrible headache, he said.

He rummaged through the medicine cabinet. I looked back at the mirror. My drooping eyelids meant I no longer looked like my brother.

I want to die, Leo said.

Everything will be better in the morning, I said.

The next day my eyelids were still droopy but the sun was shining and I took the morning off to go to the park with a book, where a pandemonium of ring-necked parakeets set their sights on my bagel but I managed to swat them away just in time.

ast night I slept for maybe a minute, said my mother. She didn't know how much longer she could keep it up. She often made comments like this and they scared me so much that I considered calling the police whenever she went a few hours without taking my phone calls.

Three and Four were now living with her. Whenever Three wanted to put her front paws on her shoulders and press her head against her cheek, my mother calmly acquiesced.

Mama, I said.

Yes.

What is your greatest dream?

My greatest dream is to be able to fly.

Come on.

Seriously, she said. I think it would be very useful to be able to hover above the world and see everything.

And not actually have to be anywhere, I said.

No, no, I would take off but I'd like to be able to land again.

Where?

On the riverbank, at the point where the river splits, in the moment he was riding there, right before he went into the water, that's where I would land, then and there.

But that moment has already happened, I said. It's impossible.

Flying is impossible too, said my mother.

One of the cats jumped onto her knees, turned around and curled up on her lap.

You asked about my dream, she said. That is my dream.

Every day, Leo would wait until I came home, and once I was home, he wouldn't have to wait long for me to leave again. He'd stopped waiting for me at night and no longer noticed if I crawled into bed next to him.

There'll be less waiting during the day as well, he said. I think you need to know that.

I was also spending all those hours at my brother's apartment waiting. Not for my brother — the dead don't just appear, they aren't real, only death is real — but for the moment my life would go on again.

In *When Women Are Friends*, the play by Hannah van Wieringen, one of the two characters said there weren't enough stories about how to deal with life after loss. For example, I know everything about how a mother could murder her children, she said, but nothing about what happens afterwards, in other words, how life continues, how people manage to get through it together. When this is the thing we're more likely to experience. Technically, there are more Tuesday afternoons where nothing really happens. In a person's life, I mean.

The audience was predominantly elderly women. It was a matinee performance, so most younger people were working, and elderly men tend not to attend performances that have the word women in the title because they think it has nothing to do with them, that women don't engage with universal issues, like how to carry on after your brother has drowned himself in a river.

One advantage of loss is that you get to put it behind you. You've lost, so you can relax and breathe again. In the weeks leading up to my brother's death, I kept wanting to open all the windows but my brother had wanted them closed. He was cold. I bought him a woollen blanket. He ordered a fan for me. I waved the fan back and forth, generating some air for myself.

In the weeks following my brother's death, I had enough oxygen but the downside of loss is that after the first few weeks there are always more weeks to come and it's difficult to adjust to the weeks continuing. And during sleepless nights you'll keep thinking that you could have got quite used to waving that fan back and forth. And there are times you'll think that breathing might not be necessary at all.

I don't want you to end your life too, said Leo one night, six months after my brother's death. I'd saved one of the stones my brother had used to drown himself and kept it in a corner of the attic. The stone had come from my mother's collection. Leo asked if we could open one of the windows. We could, it wasn't cold. And I wasn't sick, I was just sad.

On perhaps the dreariest of his final days, my brother started talking about the right to erasure. Every person has the right to be forgotten, it's the law. I asked how you could force people to forget you or if there was a company who could erase your memories while you slept, like what happened to Jim Carrey in *Eternal Sunshine of the Spotless Mind*.

You're so dumb, said my brother.

He meant, of course, your online existence. You could erase that.

I think you'll always leave traces of yourself behind, I said.

Coincidentally, I happened to know about the existence of the Wayback Machine, a digital archive that made bi-monthly screenshots of as many websites as it could. I often used it to look up old screenshots of my online shop. My brother said he'd known about the machine for ages but didn't interrupt me when I explained how it worked.

When I'm dead, he said, I want you guys to have me cremated. I don't want there to be even the slightest chance of fossil hunters digging up a piece of my skull thousands of years from now.

But humans will have wiped themselves out long before that, I said.

And I want you to send Google removal requests to every website that mentions my name.

Do it yourself, I said.

I've already started.

You know that you can't erase my memories.

He knew this.

I'll try not to think of you, I said.

When we were about twelve, my brother had a recurring nightmare. Huge grey blocks would stand all around him, so tall that he couldn't see the sky. If he had to go to the toilet in the middle of the night, the grey blocks would follow him to the bathroom. One night he came into my room with the blocks trailing behind him and crawled into bed beside me. I'm afraid, he said. He was afraid he was spineless, just like our father, and that he would develop bad breath, the sour kind that emanates from your stomach, the kind you can't do anything about, and that he would never find a job.

But you can do everything, I said. You don't have to worry.

And then he was afraid that he would always worry, even if there was no cause for concern.

One day the ringing started. I know exactly when it was, the day my brother was going to help my mother plant a rosebush. I'd driven him to the village and we were singing along to a Ween song, the one about friends being so close but so far away but then I noticed I was singing alone. I looked over and saw my brother pressing his index fingers against his ears. I thought he was playing an old game of ours, the one where he'd quickly press his ears open and closed, making everything sound like a skipping CD, so I continued singing extra loudly. Then I stopped.

My ears are ringing, he said.

He took his hands away from his ears.

It'll stop, I said. At the same moment, he said: It won't stop.

The ringing continued for the entire day. I joked it was because of my singing and he laughed but looked worried. He'd once read something about people whose ears started ringing and continued to ring for the rest of their lives. It can just randomly happen to you, he said. Like cancer.

A few days later, the ringing was still there. It wasn't a comforting sound, he said. It didn't sound like rushing water. Sometimes it turned into a beeping noise.

I wondered if something in his ears had ruptured and suggested that he should see a doctor. He nodded absently.

Don't complain if you aren't going to do anything about it, I said.

When he went to the doctor she said: There's nothing you can do about it. Sometimes it stops on its own.

See, I told you so, I said.

We were standing in front of the highest apartment building in the city, a building many people had thrown themselves off. My brother told me what happened to your body when you jump from a great height and smack onto the pavement. If you want to have any chance of surviving, then it's best to land on the balls of your feet, he said, with your knees slightly bent. And you should fall on your side rather than your back, and if that doesn't work, fall forwards with your arms covering your face. It's just that there are very few people who can survive a fall of more than thirty metres, so it's always better not to fall at all.

Promise me you'll never jump off a building, I said.

He promised.

'm always imagining how it happened, how he'd walked to the shed, grabbed his bike and taken the bike path, headed for the supermarket. At the supermarket, he turned left, riding past the therapy centre and seesaws and out of the village. He'd ridden across the fields, the sun was shining, it was early, a weekday, and there weren't many other people around. He was warm in his thick jacket. Then he turned right onto the narrow bike path. He pedalled with all his might when the path ascended, standing on the pedals until he reached the top of the hill and could see the river flowing beneath him. During the descent, he'd ridden briskly off the path, onto the grass, and into the water.

I don't know what happened after that, whether he'd fallen forwards or on his side, if he fought for his life or not, if he was afraid, if he had any thoughts, if he had, just for a moment, thought of me.

Elza wanted to know what I was going to do with my brother's ashes. I said I was going to scatter them but still had no idea where to do it.

Maybe the river, I said. Yes, probably the river, he loved it there, I think that's the right place.

I hadn't really thought about it. But I had thought about the last bag of groceries I'd brought over to him when he said he was feeling better, how he'd been reasonably positive and wide-eyed. And the packet of Oreos he never opened.

Yes, I'll throw his ashes in the drink.

And Elza said she thought it was a beautiful idea.

My brother's apartment became a warehouse for my sweaters, slippers, woollen blankets and silk scarves —I'd expanded my shop's inventory. I put little bags of lavender everywhere to keep the moths away, nothing poisonous. My brother believed that the only being he was allowed to kill was himself. The more people who chose to end their lives, the better it was for the climate, especially if it happened to be people who ate pork and showered for twenty minutes each day. The tone he used to say these things had changed over the years, shifting from reproachful to indifferent. Did you know that clownfish are going deaf because of the acidification of the ocean? he asked one day. What did you say? I replied but he held his tongue. This might have been the moment he gave up. It was around this time that he started working on his suicide note. Slept badly again, he'd written in his diary three weeks before his death. The ringing in my ears is driving me crazy. But I did start working on a letter that's difficult for me to write. It's now quarter to five and I'm feeling pretty awful. Maybe I should just eat some roasted nuts.

Three weeks before his death, he'd already known what he was going to do, that's twenty-one days of him pretending to involve me in his life. In the letter, he'd written that he loved me and that he was sorry. Sorry, he'd written. And he'd given me instructions. Don't get angry, don't fret, don't blame yourself. Don't feel stupid, I thought. Or lost, betrayed, abandoned.

L eo and I went to a barbeque hosted by some friends of ours. I was standing in the garden beside the table, sticking my hand into a bowl of tortilla chips. A man offered me a sausage.

No, thank you, I said. I'm vegetarian.

The man apologised. I said it wasn't necessary, he couldn't know what I did and didn't eat. He said that he wasn't even sure what his own wife would and wouldn't eat because it changed every week. He pointed at a woman who was standing a few metres from us, talking to two other women. She was dipping her finger into a glob of mayonnaise on her plate.

Can you ever really know everything about anyone, I asked.

The man smiled. We have twins, he said. Two boys. They know everything about each other.

I'm also a twin, I said.

Oh, how nice.

I really shouldn't say that anymore. And then I said: My brother was vegan. He drowned himself last year. He was always a little more extreme than me.

According to Elza, it would be good for me to write to him. I wrote: Dear brother, tomorrow I leave for New York, again without you. No one knows this, not our aunt, not even Leo. He's in Austria for a few weeks, taking a wood-carving masterclass with a world-famous designer whose name I keep forgetting.

I had a hard time finding the right words, and spending hours tinkering with a letter no one would read seemed pointless, so I gave up. Elza explained that I was writing the letter for myself and finding the right words could help me understand myself better but she didn't understand that for every word I wrote, I convinced myself there was a better word and that I would never find the right words.

My brother and I liked to read each other the comments people posted on online condolence registers to commemorate the dead after a tragedy. They kept writing about 'the tragedy' as if there was only one tragedy. Or they wrote that the victims had been 'killed by the tragedy'. After 9/11, someone had written: *I hope that none of you felt any pain when everything collapsed and it was raining bodies because that feels unimaginable.* But most people went with: *There are no words for this.* Or shorter still: *No words.* If you couldn't think of anything better to say than no words, then we felt it was best not to say anything at all.

y mother's father died a month after we were born, the day before our original due date. He was a mathematician, a person who loved facts, but shortly before his death, he surprised everyone by saying: I believe that feelings are the most important thing after all.

I knew him only from old photos. He had a round face, chubby belly and thin legs, like a parakeet, but if I think of him now, I always picture the British American physicist Freeman Dyson's thin face and jug ears. In an episode of the documentary series *Of Beauty and Consolation*, Dyson explained to journalist Wim Kayzer what he'd come to understand after a long scientific career was that life was about emotions, people and family.

In a way, emotions are older than intelligence, he said. They inhabit an older part of the brain. We aren't smart enough to completely understand them. For a moment I thought he'd said that emotions were the authors of intelligence but I'd misread the subtitles.

I didn't see this episode when it originally aired in 1991 but came across it in an online documentary archive. Kayzer filmed Dyson at his house in Princeton, where he read to his grandchildren and listened to what they had to say with obvious delight.

For him, life with the children is more of an intellectual adventure, said his wife, who was sitting next to him. But if they spill a little milk, it's, you know ... tougher.

Undoubtedly my children found me a bit cold, said Dyson. I don't feel cold but ... He smiled. His own parents hadn't been very affectionate either.

That's part of being human, that we have this, as far as we know, unique ability, to foresee our own deaths, he said a little later. Everybody's scared of dying, everybody's scared of getting sick. There are all sorts of things that scare me to death. Consolation mostly just comes through companionship. As soon as you somehow manage to stop thinking of yourself and start thinking of a group of people, that we're all in it together. That's the consolation, that's why I find family is of central importance.

Too late, I thought.

There is beauty and consolation in tragedy, said Dyson, not only in stories with happy endings.

I called my mother to tell her that Freeman Dyson's parents also hadn't been affectionate, and neither was he but his daughter still called him warm and caring, even if the warmth wasn't always apparent.

My mother asked what I meant. She'd just put some potatoes on to boil.

Dyson said that we understand more about the universe than our own inner world and that humankind is one of the universe's many attempts to understand itself. He says the universe is young! Everything is still starting out! God is a baby! And God understands just as little as we do about what he began!

My mother's potatoes boiled over but she called me back an hour later. It surprised me to see the word *Mother* lighting up my screen. I was the one to call her most of the time. She was familiar with Wim Kayzer's series. She remembered an episode that featured the writer John Coetzee, who had only wanted to give perfectly formulated answers, which is why he seemed perpetually lost for words. And Kayzer, who, despite Coetzee's discomfort, kept questioning him, seeking the one recollection that would be a perfect metaphor for beauty and consolation, the one anecdote that would delineate everything more clearly than a hundred theories could.

She sounded as if she was reading these words off a cheat sheet.

You should watch that episode too, she said, suddenly herself again.

Wim Kayzer and John Coetzee agreed to meet at Diaz Beach on the Cape of Good Hope, a place of significant beauty and consolation for Coetzee. On the way there, Kayzer sang an old Dutch sea shanty. *All those wanting to sail to the cape / must be bearded men / Jan, Piet, Joris and Corneel / they all have beards, they all have beards / Jan, Piet, Joris, and Corneel / They have beards, they'll sail with us!*

When we were in kindergarten, my brother and I used to sing the same song. Jampiejoris and Corneel, we sang, thinking it was about two men, not four. Jampiejoris became my brother's alter ego and would appear whenever my brother did something that wasn't allowed. When he was Jampiejoris, his voice was different, shriller. Does that mean I'm Corneel? I often asked myself. Apart from his beard I found it difficult to visualise Corneel.

Coetzee spoke about the history, flora and fauna of Diaz beach as if he was a travel guide. Every so often he'd ask Kayzer to stop filming so he could consult his notes — a small piece of paper with a couple of lines scribbled on it, which he held in his hand, just off camera.

I think it's important, even if one doesn't regularly come to a place, said Coetzee on the beach, that one should know that a place like this exists, where you can retreat, almost in a religious sense.

Coetzee found the filming of the documentary an extremely unpleasant experience, he wrote to Kayzer afterwards. Let's just wait and see how it turns out, Kayzer wrote back. Perhaps you'll see that it wasn't so bad after all. A recollection is often bleaker than the event itself.

I realised that as a child my brother had needed an alter ego to cope with his imperfections and looked up the lyrics of that old sea shanty. *All those who can't abide death and the devil / Must be bearded men*, began the last couplet. My brother had never grown a beard.

Sorry that I'm calling you again so soon, is what I intended to say when my mother picked up the phone, and I would thank her for recommending the episode with Coetzee and let her know that I understood what it was that she wasn't able to say and that I knew I talked too much and from then on I would be a silent source of consolation for her but I got her voicemail and instead rambled on about Jampiejoris and Diaz Beach and after some additional stammering, I hung up.

The Residence Inn by Marriot was just as impersonal as I'd hoped it would be. Just a tower among other towers. It was walking distance from the Sofitel, where another hedge fund investor who'd entrusted more than seven billion dollars to Bernie Madoff had jumped to his death a year ago.

The windows in my hotel room couldn't be opened. When I switched on the television, I landed in the middle of a story about President Trump's tiny hands. Someone was saying that the first documented joke about his hands had been made in 1988, exactly thirty years ago. Today was an anniversary. There was laughter. I walked over to the window and breathed onto the glass until it grew misty. Using my forefinger, I drew my brother's face. He'd been dead for two years. I stroked his cheek, which felt cold and damp. I stroked his face again and again until I'd accidentally erased it.

On weekends and during school holidays, my brother and I would drag my mattress into his room so that we could sleep together. Once in bed, we'd play our interview game. One of us was the anthropologist and the other was the interviewer. The interviewer would ask the anthropologist about the indigenous peoples he'd encountered.

Well, I was walking through the rainforest, the anthropologist explained, when I came across a man, a naked man.

A naked man, you say?

Yes, he was wearing nothing.

Absolutely nothing?

No, just a loincloth. A little cloth in front of his loins.

And that's it?

Yes, a little cloth. Nothing else.

We'd get so excited by the idea of this that we couldn't stop laughing.

was standing in front of the Freedom Tower at the World Trade Center and could see myself reflected in one of the windows by the entrance. I looked beyond the tower and then again at myself. I saw a tall woman in a long coat. Will you stop looking at yourself, my brother would always say. It was cold and the sun was setting, most of the day-trippers had already left. I asked myself what I was doing. My brother had never been here.

I'd already visited the observation deck on top of the tower using Google Maps. When I clicked on the building, I landed beside a boy and a girl whose faces were blurred. The girl's arms were wrapped around the boy's waist. He had one ordinary and one misshapen hand, a stump with half a thumb, as if the rest of his fingers had been hacked off. A firework accident perhaps. It was his right hand and maybe he was already left-handed or he might have had to learn to write with his left hand. Who would do something that stupid, my brother said to me when one of our classmates returned to school after the Christmas holidays missing two phalanges. It was the same boy who, soon after this, would put frozen dog shit on my brother's chair at school. A firecracker had exploded in his hand on New Year's Day. I remembered hearing an ambulance in the village around eleven in the morning, just as I was taking the first bite of my third beignet. The boy was asked to stand up and share his story with the class and my brother had stuck a finger in the air — the same finger that was now just a stump on that boy's hand — and said that you should never light firecrackers you found on the street, that you might as well just hack off your own finger. Now, now, said our teacher. Intentionally doing something to harm yourself strikes me as rather more problematic. And he said that Mickey Mouse also only had four fingers. Later, when my brother was being bullied, that same teacher would take him aside and tell him he should never feel he was worth less than another person, that he was unique and a very talented illustrator and that eventually, everything would fall into place.

You can't tell from looking at the footprints of the Twin Towers, two square basins in the ground, that the second tower had been slightly shorter. Both basins seemed endlessly deep and dark. I leant over to see what was happening beneath the water. I leant over a little more, hanging over the wide, bronze ledge in which the victims' names were etched, until my toes were barely touching the ground. I couldn't see anything. Careful, said someone behind me, and I quickly stood upright again. I didn't look at the woman, who was now standing beside me, peering instead at the names, all the people who had worked in the towers, who had perhaps jumped because they wanted to determine their own fate. Out of the corner of my eye, I watched as the woman placed a rose by one of the names and felt ashamed because my belly had just been lying on top of it. Sorry, I said, and the woman nodded briefly.

It was incredibly windy as I walked back to my hotel. It was spring but it felt like autumn. I buried my nose in the collar of my lambswool sweater. Americans don't like woollen sweaters, they prefer fleece. I wanted to eat vegetarian hamburgers in my room and watch the latest season of *Survivor* with ketchup smeared all over my chin. I wanted to disappear, then come back again.

A man stood on a desert island.

Thirty-nine days! he shouted. Twenty people! One survivor!

It was Jeff Probst, the host.

In this competition, everything rests on your ability to make the right decision at the right moment, he called out to the twenty contestants who had just washed up on the island. And the competition starts now!

Wearing tight grey pants and black lace-up shoes, contestant Chris was walking through the rainforest searching for something to eat. I'm a model, he said to the camera, but I'm going to keep that to myself for now, because withholding information is important in *Survivor*. His opponent Libby, a consultant, wore a bra and ruffled lace hotpants. Sebastian was a fisherman and he was wearing black Hawaiian-print boxers.

My brother and I used to watch American *Survivor* at home. We'd binge-watch entire seasons on Sundays. It was only at the end of each episode, once my face finally relaxed, that I would realise how intently I'd been watching. We couldn't stop watching, especially when the contestants were arguing, gossiping, or when they said they *haven't come to make friends* only to cry when another player betrayed them. What an overreaction, my brother would shout. He was convinced that the Americans were just acting, and this wasn't necessarily a bad thing, as long as they kept it credible. We did our best to comprehend the characters, interpreting their movements, their glances and how they formulated their lies. We were anthropologists and they were the savages, wearing loincloths that stylists had selected with care.

In spite of her hot-pink bra, financial consultant Laurel knew how to fly under the radar. She formed an alliance with three other contestants, which is how she managed to survive round after round. When the contestants had family visits after thirty-one days on the island, Laurel embraced her brother and revealed her true feelings for the first time. It's been so hard without him, she tearfully explained to Jeff. You can't trust anyone in this competition but I can always count on him.

What an overreaction, I said, slamming my laptop shut in frustration.

My phone woke me in the middle of the night. Leo was calling. It was almost seven o'clock in Austria, dinner time. I sat up in bed and tried to sound coherent.

How are things over there, Leo asked. Are you home or at your brother's place?

Home, I said.

It's raining there, isn't it, he said.

It might be. I haven't been outside today.

You have windows, don't you?

Yes, I said. Yes, it's raining.

Hinrich thinks that my vulvas are worthy of international acclaim, said Leo.

Hinrich, the Austrian designer whose name I kept forgetting.

That's great! I said. Hinrich is right.

I pictured him on the telephone in the hotel lobby, pacing back and forth, how he couldn't wait to share his news with me, and to feel closer to him I pressed the telephone nearer to my ear. When we hung up, I walked over to the window and looked out over Sixth Avenue. It was indeed raining here too.

I want to compete against the best of them in the finale, the muscular male participants in both the American and Dutch versions of *Survivor* always say. When they say the best of them, they mean the other muscular men in the competition. The guys who are constantly lugging wood and trekking through the jungle with machetes to prove how strong they are. It's only once they've beaten these guys in a challenge that they feel they have truly won. But the best survivors aren't muscular and fearless, they are frightened and small and seek the protection of others because anyone who works alone is lost.

My brother's life was a series of poor *Survivor* decisions but the stupidest thing he did was break his alliance with the only other contestant he could trust, the one who would have given him her last grains of rice, who would have carried him on her back to the finish line if it came to that.

ne out of every three thousand pigs is born without an anus, said my brother. Compared to one out of every five thousand people. Did you know that?

I didn't know that.

The anusless pigs are used for experimental research aimed at finding a cure for the anusless people.

We watched an Italian film about a dog trainer. The trainer had two shepherd dogs and a miniature pig that ran around everywhere, between the table legs and dogs' legs, and through the remnants of a plate of spaghetti that had fallen on the floor.

There's this German miniature pig, said my brother. A cross between a Vietnamese breed and an American breed, mixed with German blood. They do experiments on it too.

The dog trainer hung himself. We saw the two leather boots twitching. Underneath them, the tiny pig snuffled around the overturned chair.

All the pigs in the world, even wild pigs, end up being consumed, said my brother.

What do you think of those boots? I asked.

was looking through my mother's old photo albums. In almost every photo taken before we turned ten, my brother and I were touching: lying on top of each other, walking arm in arm or holding each other's hands. But not after that. On our eleventh birthday, we stood next to each other in front of the house. We were both wearing party hats attached to elastic bands that looped under our chins. There was a tense grin on my face and I was sticking two fingers up behind my brother's head. My brother was smiling vaguely and his eyes were dull. Ever since he turned nine, the same year he was bullied at school, my brother's eyes had gradually got duller. That particular afternoon, he'd wanted to read his *Spike and Suzy* comics, this I still remember. He hadn't wanted to be there. My father had taken the photo, he was still around then. He hadn't wanted to be there either.

hat will happen to poetry when seasons cease to exist? the poet pondered. I looked at my brother. His eyes were locked on the poet. *The Labrador*, she was now saying. This was the title of a poem without seasons. She read it aloud and the audience listened in silence and I looked at my brother again and this time he was looking back at me. We burst into laughter. We were silently shaking with laughter. The auditorium seating was shaking along with us.

After the reading, once we were standing outside and the first drops of a heavy autumn rainstorm had just announced themselves, my brother asked if our laughter during the reading was anxious laughter. I said that it wasn't, because I understood the urgent nature of climate change and still wasn't scared of it, and my brother said I was the only person he knew who could face humanity's uncertain future without any fear. There was admiration in his voice and I felt proud, even though I knew quite well that I wasn't so brave, not like him. When I think of my brother in his final years, I like to think of this moment, when he still had some space for me, between all of the downpours.

Simon van Collem was a Dutch broadcast journalist who, up until his death in 1989, hosted various TV shows in which he reviewed films, attended premieres and interviewed Hollywood stars, all while sounding as though he was perpetually out of breath. My father liked to do impressions and Van Collem was his speciality. The trick, he'd say, is to begin by exhaling completely and only then start to talk. We weren't familiar with Van Collem, so we didn't think much of it. Still, my father kept impersonating him, even if we were his only audience. After his death, my brother started doing his own impressions. I laughed so hard at his impression of Dad doing Simon van Collem that my mother kept coming out of her bedroom with her face all crumpled. Among his things we found a videotape containing episodes of Van Collem's last show. We listened to his voice with our eyes closed, picturing our father's face, the way he would sit at the breakfast table with his lips pursed and keep on talking until he was gasping for breath. And we found it very calming.

Elza sat with her back to the window in her study. The light shining through the window was bright and I could only see her silhouette, her hair piled high on her head. A strand of hair had come loose and was sticking out from her right temple, bobbing along as she spoke. That morning I'd read that shortly before Primo Levi threw himself down a flight of stairs, he'd written to his English translator saying that he had felt better when he was at Auschwitz. At Auschwitz he'd been young and still believed in things.

Can I ask you something?

Yes, sure, said Elza.

Did your parents want to go on living after the war?

I think so but they weren't quite sure how they were supposed to do it. My mother survived Bergen-Belsen by staying out of sight. Even after the war she remained in hiding, it just never ended.

So, there are people who can go through something like that and still manage to keep going, I said. Why couldn't my brother do it?

I don't know if your brother really *chose* to die, said Elza. Depression can make a person incredibly despondent.

The body is a vessel for the soul, said Stijn, the yoga instructor. Back when my brother still believed in all kinds of things — in the benefit of sweat lodge ceremonies, and Osho's integrity — Stijn would occasionally come to stay the night with him and he would always remove his shoes and socks at the door. Stijn had endured a long journey, from chaos to peace, and violence to love. Sometimes he'd bring an avocado with him and then cut it into slices on a plate.

In the tearoom at the crematorium, Stijn embraced me with his entire body. You can tell how intimately two people are connected by the way that they embrace and the distance between their hips. Ever since reading this I always made sure I pressed my hips firmly against Leo's when I put my arms around him. Stijn held me for so long that I forgot all about my hips. He said that my brother had only ever looked happy when he was sleeping.

Like a little pig, he said. So sweet.

Pigs are intelligent and empathic animals, I said. But they aren't very happy.

lza asked how things were going with Leo and me.

Better, I said. Leo has cleaned up his workshop and he's getting a lot of work.

And you? she asked.

I'm still spending a lot of time at my brother's place. I'm reading his diaries for the second time. There's not much in them, especially towards the end, it's just all factual accounts. What he did each day, how much medicine he'd taken. Maybe I'm overlooking something.

What are you looking for?

I'm trying to understand him. When someone says they love you but still ends up leaving, I can't understand it. I don't believe in that kind of love.

What kind of love do you believe in?

I don't know. The kind where you stay together.

Elza asked if I still loved Leo.

Of course I still love Leo, I said.

During the time that the mouse was around, my brother wrote (MOUSE) above every diary entry. The mouse chewed holes in his bananas. In the meantime, my brother would lie in his bed with his heart pounding. He wasn't afraid of the mouse. He was afraid that he wouldn't be able to empty the attic, there were still so many comic books and video games up there. I suggested taking them to the charity shop but he wanted to destroy them. Everything had to go, the world was buckling under the weight of our possessions. The fact that reusing things was far better for the environment than destroying them didn't seem to get through to him. His paranoia superseded his factual knowledge: our possessions were boxing us in.

The mouse wasn't afraid of the cats. At night, Three and Four slept on their cushions by the window and the mouse would leave them little droppings on the windowsill. One morning, my brother found the mouse in the bottom of an almost empty jar of honey he'd forgotten to close. He took the jar and walked over to the park to set him free. The mouse had trouble freeing itself from the stickiness at the bottom of the jar. My brother had to give it a hand and he could easily have been bitten and suffered all the serious consequences of this, because mice carry viruses that can shut down your kidneys, but the mouse didn't bite him and a few days later my brother died of something else entirely.

My mother wanted to keep him at home, in the living room, behind the sofa, because we never used that space anyway. Except there was a large mirror hanging on the wall so whenever you walked into the room you would see my brother twice, lying in the open casket wearing his blue sweater. When they brought him inside, his hair had been slicked back too neatly. No one was doing anything about it, so I went over and carefully raked my fingers through it. For a moment, I stroked his cheek and it felt as if I was stroking his leather sofa, the part that was a little less worn.

My mother put a stuffed animal beside his head, something that resembled a grey mouse with red buttons for eyes. The girl who lived next door had made it. When my mother left the room, I took the mouse out of the coffin and placed it next to the condolence cards on the bookshelf. It was only after reading the pre-printed sentiments on those cards that I started to cry. *No longer among us but never far from our hearts. In the eyes of the world, he was just one person but to us, he was the whole world.*

My mother's gardening club arrived, along with her walking club. I filled their glasses and put a selection of cheeses on the table. If my brother could only have seen me walking with those trays, how skilfully I handled it all. For a while I thought about this every day. If only he could see me now. But it wasn't as if I actually believed he was watching me from above.

H is old friends from the bar carried his coffin into the chapel on their shoulders. They walked very slowly, perfectly synchronised, like soldiers. After the cremation, we had drinks in my mother's garden and an old man approached me saying he was my great-uncle Gijsbert. I asked him how he was doing. Good, he said, although he'd recently had heart surgery and was still recovering. My mother's uncle Ed was there too. He was having some issues with his knees.

Once everyone had left and I'd cleaned up all the glasses, I noticed my mother standing by the kitchen window, which looked out onto the street. She stood with her back to me, her arms hanging limply beside her body.

Mama, I said.

She nodded gravely but I wasn't sure if she'd heard me. I threw my arms around her like a warm sweater and felt her flinch.

Just let me be for a moment, she said softly.

My mother said that her son had died of a sickness, as if he hadn't chosen to leave us. I knew that depression was a sickness. Maybe it was the depression that sent him into the water. It had told my brother that he wasn't the one who was sick but life was. Life itself was sick. When people asked, my mother would say that she had lost her husband to a cerebral haemorrhage. She was well aware that he'd left her long before that actually happened. Being the one who leaves guarantees that you won't be the one who is left. My mother has never been left. She was gone long before I was born.

Think about the old days, I said. When everything was good.

My brother was lying with his head in my lap again and I was massaging his temples.

When was it good? he asked. It was never good.

You must have at least one good memory, I said.

I tried to recall situations, moments in which we'd been happy but I couldn't come up with anything. My mind was empty. I could remember a feeling, a certain unity that hadn't been there later, when we were twenty-eight and he'd gone to Brazil, or earlier, when he had his interview for the art college. Or even earlier than that. I closed my eyes, stopped massaging and tried to stop my thoughts.

Elza said that I should just say whatever I was thinking to others, the way I used to, when things were bad but not quite broken.

No offence, I always said to my brother when I'd just offended him.

You can ruin a lot of things with words, I said now.

Elza believed it was important to talk.

If only your brother had spoken a little more.

I said that I hadn't given him the space to do so. I'd spoken too much and failed to understand his silences in time.

elp, I said. I was lying in bed and said this softly, so that it wouldn't wake Leo. Help, I repeated. I stepped out of bed and walked into the living room, over to the window. Help, I whispered to the window. Outside, a student was bending over her bike. She was searching for something on the ground and almost fell over a few times. Help, I said to the girl with the bike, and the plant on the windowsill, and the Moroccan cushion on the sofa. I picked up the cushion and held it to my face. Help, I whispered. If you don't want to be helped you should definitely call out for help, said the man who was teaching the emergency response class my brother organised for the employees at the bar. There had been space for one more participant, so I'd been allowed to join the class. The word *help* scares people, said the man. They don't want to be drawn into someone else's drama.

I looked outside again. The student had climbed onto her bike and was riding slowly towards the park, where one night I'd had a full cup of 7Up flung at my face by a rowdy teenage girl who happened to be passing by with a group of friends. I walked over to her with my face dripping. You're brave enough to do this with all your friends around, I said. But if I ever catch you here alone, I'll get you.

I was amazed at myself, how threatening this sounded. My words left a thrilling silence in their wake, and then the girls burst into laughter. As I was walking away, I heard one of them doing an impression of me with an exaggerated posh accent and a high-pitched voice.

Watch out, I whispered to the student who was swaying as she disappeared through the iron park gates and I recalled how my brother, in his Jampiejoris phase, would open doors by throwing himself against them, the same way he kept fearlessly throwing himself into the world. Then I pictured him standing in the corner of the playground at school, wearing a beanie over his damp curls, which meant that they would remain plastered to his forehead for the rest of the day. I had forgotten how he stood there every morning that year, trying to catch my eye while I kept looking the other way, afraid of being drawn into that drafty corner for all eternity. What I remember most vividly from my time at primary school is fear. I didn't know what I needed to do to appear normal and when my brother didn't seem to know either I felt I'd lost my last anchor. A kind of neediness crept into his demeanour and I found this unsettling. He was the stronger of the two of us, he bossed me around at home and I complained about it but I bore his contempt better than his weakness. He had to look after me because no one else would. I suddenly remembered how he'd sit behind his computer at the kitchen table, years later, after dropping out of his English studies, when he'd tentatively started doing computer animation again. I was standing beside him. He looked up at me, with those familiar helpless eyes, and I had quickly looked away to focus on the figure moving across the screen, a 3D animation in a completely new style. He wanted me to share my initial impression of it. His eyes bore into my cheek and his nervous, shaky leg kept banging against the table and I felt myself withdrawing, growing so cold inside that I had trouble making any kind of sound. Eventually, I mumbled something that made him sink deeper into his chair. When he clicked the animation away, I understood that I was supposed to say something warm, something constructive, but couldn't. I was frozen. And that's something else I hadn't considered. My brother never asked me why I didn't help him.

You have to shout *fire* if you want help, said the man at the emergency response training. Fire affects everyone. People will always spring into action if there's a fire. He was a former fireman and after years of service could no longer hear high-pitched sounds. He didn't respond to anything I said.

'd forgotten that Leo had invited people over, two co-workers who shared his workshop. They were sitting at the kitchen table when I came home. Leo was stirring a pot of tomato soup. He was wearing his good shirt.

Sorry I'm so late, I said. There were loads of orders today.

His co-workers asked about my sweaters, so I opened my laptop and showed them my web shop. The female co-worker immediately said that she wanted the Icelandic cardigan. But I want that one too, said the male co-worker, and I told him that I had an extra cardigan lying around that wasn't listed on the website, a blue one. He could have it if he wanted. It had belonged to my brother but I didn't mention that.

I was feeling good. It was the perfect time for my neo-Brit-glam-rock playlist, so I put on the music and we ate soup and drank red wine, so much wine that we began singing loudly along to the songs, even Leo, with his arms spread wide open. I let myself fall into his lap, almost fell off it and then it was time for me to throw up.

In the bathroom, I vomited red and purple. Leo knocked on the door and I said I was fine, that it would soon be over. After a few minutes, my stomach was completely empty. When I walked back into the kitchen, I could hear my own voice emanating from the speaker. The voice was saying that she'd recently bought two kettles, one for Leo and one for herself, for the future, for when they would break up. Elza's voice asked if I wanted to leave Leo. I quickly switched off the speaker.

Once the colleagues had left, Leo started furiously washing the dishes.

I always record my therapy sessions, I said.

He didn't turn around.

The answer was no, I said. I don't want to leave you. I gave the other kettle to my mother.

Leo put a soup bowl on the drying rack.

I want us to be together, I said. It's just that I don't really know how to do that.

So what!

He hurled the dish brush into the soapy waters and gripped the edge of the countertop.

You don't always need to know exactly how to do something before you do it, he said.

As I remember it, we had just turned four when our parents rented a large holiday apartment on the sea. They usually rented a house in a secluded area but they'd wanted my brother and me to be able to play with other children for once. The only other child I can recall is this French girl from the apartment next door who was always frowning at us.

One afternoon I walked into our apartment with my little bucket full of shells when suddenly I noticed strange jackets hanging in the hallway. I opened the living room door and where the sofa usually was stood a table with a vase of flowers on it, neither of which had been there that morning. I shut that door, opened another, and found the French girl lying in my bed. She looked angry and yelled something at me, so I quickly shut the door again. But I didn't know where to go, so I just stood in the hallway with all the doors closed. Behind them, everything appeared the same but nothing was the same. Eventually, one of the doors opened, the door that led outside, and my brother, who'd heard me crying, yelled, What are you doing here, grabbed me by the arm and pulled me out into the corridor. I still remember how it felt to stand in that hallway. It's how I feel now that my brother is gone, the only difference being that he's no longer here to pull me out of it.

dreamed that I saw him again. But I can only make it on Tuesday, he said. That was good enough for me. I could live with that.

Some Wikipedia pages I read only because I knew the information on them would interest my brother. I searched for facts about pigs and deforestation and antidepressants so that I could share these little titbits with him, always in small doses, otherwise it would seem like I deliberately sought them out. After his death, there was no limit to my googling. I constantly searched for new facts, for ways to outsmart my brother, now that it was no longer necessary. I learned that pigs will compulsively rub against the bars of their excessively narrow cages in a desperate attempt to seek out some form of contact.

o you remember when we'd just met? I asked. When you were still living in that little room above the social enterprise workshop.

Yes, said Leo.

You had a new wooden floor and you were constantly mopping it.

I never mopped, said Leo.

We were lying in bed. It was Sunday morning. I lay my head on his chest to listen to his heart, then flopped back onto my own pillow. Leo grabbed his telephone from the bedside table.

Trump isn't a climate change denier anymore, he said after a while.

We watched a video of the president admitting that the climate was changing but it would get better on its own. He wasn't going to spend billions saving it.

My brother was right, I said. It's not going to get any better.

Leo sighed and stepped out of bed.

Come back, I said, but he'd already put on his trousers and was mumbling something about making coffee.

I wanted to say I was mistaken. Dear Leo, it will get better, is what I wanted to say. Maybe not on its own but it will get better.

He looked at me.

Corry's out, I said.

Who? asked Leo.

Corry Konings. From Dutch *Survivor*. She lost a challenge to Johnny Kraaijkamp junior.

I don't understand why you watch that rubbish.

Now it's just a question of whether Johnny will make it to the Tribal Merge.

Are you sleeping here or over there tonight?

Over there, I said.

Maybe you should just move into your brother's place, said Leo. He's been dead for two and a half years and you're still spending more time there than you are here. How many times are you going to read through his diaries?

Jesus. You're in a bad mood.

Yeah, he said.

Then I watched as something erupted inside of him, his face turned red.

I've had it! he shouted. Either come back to me or stay over there. Just make a choice.

He looked like he was going to kick a hole in the door. For a moment he reminded me of my brother. Then he picked up his shirt from the floor and sniffed it.

arcel was wearing a suit and had a telephone at his ear. He stopped in his tracks when I greeted him and stood there signalling that I should wait.

Yes. Yes. Yes, he said into the telephone. Sorry.

And after a short silence again: Sorry, something's come up. I have to go now.

Sorry, he said to me. There's stress at work. He put his hand to his mouth and pulled a startled face to demonstrate the panic. Then, abruptly, he stopped and his expression turned serious.

I knew that look. Since my brother's death, people were always giving me that look. Next he was going to ask me how I was doing.

It's been ages! I shrieked.

Yes, sorry, he said, for not coming to his cremation.

I said that it didn't matter. I asked how he was doing. He said he was working on a project aimed at getting more city dwellers to separate their recycling.

It's all about motivating people, he said. Fascinating stuff.

You need to make it sexy.

Exactly! he said, then the serious look returned.

How are you?

I said I was good, that I separated paper and glass but didn't separate my food and garden waste. And I've read his diaries, I said. There's not a lot in them but he did write a few things about you, he wrote that he really loved you, even though he left you, and that it was possible to love someone and still leave them. He didn't know *how* it was possible. No one knew that, the way no one knows what is at the centre of the earth because there is a thick, impenetrable shell all around it, is how he explained it. These aren't my words, I added and hoped he couldn't see in my eyes that they were my words, the only ones I could give him. I told him about a bridge in Scotland that dogs threw themselves off in a trance-like state, only to plummet to their deaths on the rocks below. On average, one dog a month jumped off the bridge and no one could make any sense of that either. There are some things we just don't know, I said. But your tarte Tatin was the most delicious thing he'd ever tasted because he wrote about that too. (I wasn't making up that part.) I said it was only now that I understood my brother had been searching for something he couldn't find in his family. This angered me but I could also understand it, in the same way that Leo was mad at me but also understood why I always ran to my brother's apartment. I've stopped running now, I said, because it is possible to love someone and not leave them. Sorry I'm talking too much. One day I'm going to stop saying sorry quite so often, by the way.

Ah, said Marcel, my tarte Tatin.

His eyes grew misty. His telephone rang. Shit, he said.

Go on, answer it, I said.

I patted his arm for a moment, then we continued on our way. She's still alive, he's still alive, I thought every time someone walked by. She didn't throw herself in front of a train. Everyone who's still alive clearly thinks life is worth living. Clearly, I think life is worth living.

n idle moments, like when I'm waiting for the tram, I feel myself landing in my body. It's not the same as falling. First I feel my legs, then my feet, then the ground. And then I stand firmly, like someone who understands her purpose in the world.

A toddler in China survived a landslide that followed torrential rain because her grandmother had got on her hands and knees and bent over her like an arch. The grandmother hadn't survived the landslide, so if you have a sturdy table, it might be better to shield yourself with that. And if there is no shelter to be found, roll yourself into a tiny ball, protect your head, and seek refuge in yourself.

Acknowledgements

The passages on Josef Mengele and the chapter about Tibi and Miki Offer were inspired by *Josef Mengele, nazi-arts: zijn leven en misdaden* by Anders Otte Stensager (Ad. Donker, 2010) and *Children of the Flames: Dr. Josef Mengele and the Untold Story of the Twins of Auschwitz* by Lucette Lagnado and Sheila Cohn Dekel (William Morrow, 1990).